She reached over and turned his face toward hers with her palm. His breath rushed out of him with surprise. Her movements were bold, yet her touch was soft and caring.

"Just say what's in your heart," she whispered.

When she released his face, his emotions were churning and he felt as if she'd opened his eyes to what had been there all along. He just couldn't see it.

Without thinking, he cupped his hand around her neck and the world seemed to disappear as he closed his eyes and guided her lips to his. They tasted of ripe peaches, a sun-radiant burst of glorious wonder.

His movements were tentative at first. He wanted to focus on her, rather than on the intense need she drove within him.

The need to devour.

She leaned into him, kissing back unrestrained, and he wanted to shout with joy. The tip of his tongue dipped into her mouth and she groaned. Opened deeper. So he slid inside and discovered a velvety, warm place he wanted to explore forever.

Abruptly, he ended the kiss and leaned back in his seat.

"I just wanted to show you what was in my heart," he said in a low voice.

Books by Harmony Evans

Harlequin Kimani Romance

Lesson in Romance
Stealing Kisses

HARMONY EVANS

loves writing sexy, emotional, contemporary love stories. *Stealing Kisses* is her second novel for Harlequin Kimani Romance.

Her debut novel, *Lesson in Romance,* received 4½ stars from *RT Book Reviews.* Harmony also earned two prestigious nominations in her first year of publication. She was a "Debut Author of the Year" finalist for the Romance Slam Jam 2013 Emma Awards. In addition, she was a 2012 RT Reviewers' Choice Awards Double-Finalist ("First Series Romance" and "Kimani Romance").

Harmony is currently busy penning more novels for Harlequin Kimani. Visit her at www.harmonyevans.com, on Facebook, or follow @harmonyannevans for the latest news on upcoming releases.

STEALING *Kisses*

HARMONY EVANS

In loving memory of Carol Butler Jackson

(April 20, 1930–June 2, 2012)

I miss you, Mommy. You were always a star to me.

Recycling programs
for this product may
not exist in your area.

ISBN-13: 978-0-373-86330-3

STEALING KISSES

For questions and comments about the quality of this book, please contact us at CustomerService@Harlequin.com.

Printed in U.S.A.

Dear Reader,

I'm fascinated by famous sports stars. Not so much what's written about them in the headlines, but more by what's left out.

Derek Lansing is living a dream life. But there's a price to pay for his rise to fame in the sports world. He's estranged from his dad and brother—the two people who supported him from the very beginning.

He wants to reunite with them, but pride prevents him from taking the first step. Can he let down his guard and allow life coach Natalie Kenyon help him right his past wrongs before it's too late? Along the way, Derek and Natalie explore a passion that is powerful, rhythmic and unforgettable.

I hope you enjoy reading *Stealing Kisses* as much as I enjoyed writing it. I'd love to hear from you. Feel free to email me at harmonyevans@roadrunner.com.

Be blessed,

Harmony Evans

Chapter 1

For the first time in her life Natalie Kenyon wished she was late. The explosive echo of the basketball sounded like a dire warning as she stood inside the New York Skylarks practice court.

Whether it was doing her own taxes or carefully screening any man who wanted to date her, Natalie left nothing to chance, especially where her heart was concerned.

She was always on time and always in control.

The *thump-thump* of the basketball intensified, reminding Natalie that she was here for one reason: to change Derek Lansing's life.

She was sure Derek would be like the rest of her clients: wildly successful, yet highly inefficient in their day-to-day lives. As a life coach she advised her A-list clientele on everything from time management and goal-setting to relationships and intimacy. She loved her job and she was good at it.

Then why was her stomach churning as it used to before a big competition? The former professional ice-skater chastised herself for being nervous.

"Ridiculous," Natalie muttered. "He's just another client."

Peering around a row of seats, she caught a glimpse of the popular basketball star and clamped her hand over her mouth in shock.

Derek was shooting baskets with such ferocity it was as though his whole life depended on making every shot. The man was an island. His eyes were totally focused on the net, on the goal.

Yet her eyes were all over him.

He was tall, perhaps six feet six inches, and lean-muscled with rich dark brown skin that glistened with sweat. His shoulder-length jet-black dreadlocks swayed rhythmically with his every movement, teasing her imagination.

When he grabbed the last ball from the cart, he yelled something she couldn't understand. His legs, powerfully built and tense with virile energy, sprung into the air, seeming to master space and time.

She held her breath, her eyes following the arc of the ball to its final destination. But at the last moment it missed the net, slammed the backboard and bounced to the floor, rolling in her direction.

Derek swung off the rim, landed on the floor,

grabbed his knees and howled. The pain in that sound went straight to her heart. She recognized it.

It was the sound of desperation, of a soul cracked wide open and laid bare to an empty room that couldn't judge, couldn't laugh.

So this is Derek Lansing, Natalie thought. Number seventeen. Star forward for the New York Skylarks.

She adjusted her purse, checked her watch and smiled. She was right on schedule.

Time to turn his world upside down.

Natalie walked out onto the court and stopped the basketball with the heel of her black stiletto boot.

"Looking for this?" she asked, one hand on her hip to steady herself.

Derek uncurled his body, slow and easy, like a bear emerging from hibernation. He stood still, chest heaving, and her heart raced as his eyes slid down her legs and traveled back up her body.

Under the bright lights, her right eye twitched involuntarily and she realized with horror that he probably thought she was winking at him. She dropped the diva pose and almost lost her balance, but quickly regained it.

He strode over to her, his face like stone.

"This is a private practice. No fans allowed."

He sounded irritated and she realized he was probably embarrassed that he'd missed the shot.

Yet his eyes, gray and thick-lashed, rounded her face with keen interest. "Not even beautiful ones."

Warmth flooded her body at his compliment, although she knew he probably didn't mean it to sound as intimate as it did.

"Where's the guard?" he muttered, looking over her head toward the door.

She laughed, releasing some of her nervousness. "Do I look dangerous to you?"

His eyes seemed to take possession of her curves as they roamed her body again, leaving a trail of fire.

His lips tilted up. "Depends on which part you're talking about."

She crossed her arms over her chest, her stiletto boot barely teetering on the ball. "Excuse me?"

With no response, he pulled up his shirt and she almost fell off the ball again, but he only wiped the sweat from his face.

A rush of desire poured through her at the sight of his abdomen, cut deep with muscles, and she wondered what it would feel like if her tongue were to take a slow ride in the deep valleys of his rich brown skin.

Oh, Lord, it had been so long since she'd touched a man.

She moistened her lips involuntarily just as he stepped forward, gathering his locks into a low ponytail, and her face heated again.

"Well?" he said, peering down at her.

He was so close, only an arm's length away. The urge to reach out and touch his skin, glistening with sweat, was so strong she barely heard him.

He poked her on the shoulder. "Are you going to give it to me or am I going to have to play you for it?"

Caught off guard, her head snapped up. "What are you talking about?"

Her eyes darted up to his face where amusement danced in his gray eyes.

He pointed at her foot. "How about a little one-on-one?" he teased. "Fan against man."

Her eyes widened and she looked away. The meeting was not going according to plan. It had been a while since a man had rendered her completely speechless, both in his looks and his manner. He'd thrown her for a loop, but now it was time to get things back under her control.

Trying to avoid looking at his muscular legs, she bent her knees as gracefully as her black pencil skirt would allow and picked up the ball. After adjusting her purse, she placed the ball snugly within the crook of her left arm.

"Mr. Lansing. We have a meeting that was supposed to start—" she checked her watch and frowned "—two minutes ago. I am not a fan and I am most certainly not here to play games. I'm here to discuss the rules of engagement and the clock is ticking."

Derek placed his hand over his chest, his eyes absorbing hers like a secret told under the covers. "I didn't know we were getting married," he replied.

The intimacy in his tone stirred an intense yearning and a long-held dream, neither of which would likely be fulfilled.

Natalie was used to denying her needs to focus on the task at hand, but she was finding it very difficult to concentrate in front of this way-too-gorgeous man.

She lifted her chin. "Not married, Mr. Lansing. Organized. Your manager called me this morning and I came right over. He said you needed a little help."

Derek burst out laughing. "Wow, when I told Tony I needed a personal assistant, I was just joking. I never thought he'd actually hook me up with one."

Natalie clutched the ball tighter, bristling inside. "I am not your personal assistant," she replied in a terse tone. "I am your life coach."

He clasped his hands loosely on his hips. "What's the difference?"

She smiled, happy to provide a definition. "Easy. A personal assistant is at your beck and call. She or he runs around doing everything you want. A life coach helps you set goals so you can manage your time and your life more efficiently."

His doubtful look irked her to the core, so it was time to break it down to brass tacks.

"I'm not your go-for, Mr. Lansing. I'm your life-saver."

He raised a brow, and it was clear he was trying not to laugh again.

"Oh-h. Now you're talking my language. My favorite flavor is orange. What flavor are you?"

She exhaled so hard the ball almost popped out of her grasp. Pushing aside her frustration, she looked into his eyes and nearly smiled at what she saw. One twinkled with mischief, the other with mayhem. Clearly the man enjoyed stirring up a fuss, making her crazy with something she'd rather not think about right now.

"Can you be serious, please?" she huffed, forcing the ball back into place.

He shrugged indifferently and then walked around her in a circle making imaginary free throws.

"How can I be serious when you haven't even told me your name?"

Now it was her turn to be embarrassed. How could she have forgotten something as simple as an introduction? No wonder things were so out of her control.

"Sorry. I'm Natalie Kenyon," she said, fishing a business card out of her purse. "I own a company called StarCoach, Inc. I help my clients with time management, organization and motivation."

He stopped walking and his fingertips leaned against hers for the briefest of moments as he took the card from her grasp. After a quick glance, he stuck it into the waistband of his navy-blue basketball shorts and wrested the ball from her grasp.

"Thanks. But the only thing I need to keep track of is right here in my hands."

He spun the basketball on his index finger, and kept it going with the other hand. "My whole world revolves around the game. It's all that matters to me."

She crossed her arms and, with a twinge of guilt, took aim.

"That's not what the headlines say."

Derek flinched and swung his head toward hers. The ball dropped to the floor with a loud twang and he grabbed it before it bounced a second time.

Natalie knew she'd hit a nerve, but sometimes she had to play hard, especially when a client was as stubborn as Derek seemed to be.

"Oh, yeah?" He smirked. "What's the latest?"

She met his eyes, spoke softly. "That you're on a three-game suspension for not showing up at morning practices for the past month. You've been irresponsible, unfocused and like a different person—both on and off the court."

Derek bounced the ball a few times, a bored expression on his face.

"They fit all that in a headline?"

She tapped her foot rapidly. As attractive as he was, he was really testing her patience this morning.

"You don't seem to be taking this situation very seriously," she said in a calm voice.

He shrugged and bounced the ball again. "Would you?"

"Absolutely," she said, nodding. In fact, she took everything seriously. It was one of her worst faults. Behind her calm and poised demeanor, she was a bundle of nervous energy that was never satisfied.

His face went hard, but there was pain in his eyes. "Then you must care what people think about you. Thankfully, I don't have that problem."

One massive hand palmed the ball and he pointed it at her. "So you can just take your Gucci purse, and all the little motivational brochures you probably got stuffed in there, on down to Wall Street. With this economy, those guys need it more than I do."

Her heart sank, but she was intrigued rather than dismayed by his attitude. Derek wasn't a typical A-lister. Instead of soaking up the adoration of his fans, Derek seemed almost resentful of the attention. The psychologist in her wanted to know why.

A memory slashed her brain, rocked her back into the past. She'd been in his place before. Esteemed and highly regarded one minute, forgotten and scorned the next. She could help him before it was too late. If he would only let her.

She took a chance, reached out and touched his arm. It was thick with tension. "I'm not here about me," she said quietly. "I'm here for you."

He took a couple of steps back, as if she was offering something that would hurt rather than help him.

The playfulness on his face was gone and his voice was like stone again.

"And I'm here to play ball. No more. No less. And as much as I would love to stand here and stare at that pretty face of yours, I've got to get back to the court."

And with a squeak of his sneaker, he turned and walked away, dribbling the ball and whistling as though he didn't have a care in the world.

But he wasn't fooling her. She knew how easy it was to pretend.

Derek was supertalented, handsome and wealthy. But even without a degree in psychology, Natalie could tell that beneath the bad-boy attitude was a man who was in pain. It was clear he would require a different, nontraditional approach to get him on board with her plan.

Checking her watch, she mentally ticked off the to-do items on her schedule for the rest of the day, and decided she could squeeze in some minor inconvenience.

As quietly as she could, she set her purse on the floor and slowly unzipped her boots. After a brief glance around to make sure she was alone, she pulled off her panty hose and unbuttoned the top button of her shirt.

With a quick toe flex, she sprinted like a gazelle toward Derek and stole the ball from him middribble. She rounded him for the layup and, mercifully, the ball went up, over and through the basket.

She caught it and passed it to Derek so hard he nearly dropped the ball. She wanted to laugh out loud at the surprised look on his face.

"What's the matter?" she teased, shifting her bare feet back and forth, ready to charge forth. "You said you wanted to play one-on-one, didn't you?"

Derek dribbled the ball a few times and she could tell he was doing his best to appear unruffled by the sudden change in her appearance, and her attitude.

"I thought you were leaving."

Her toes curled as she felt his eyes move over her bare legs and feet. The ball whizzed through the air and she caught it from him easily.

She crossover-dribbled the ball, keeping her feet planted on the cold wood floor, as she tried to anticipate his next move.

"I never back away from a challenge," she said, dribbling the ball.

For a moment the only sound in the room was the twang-twang of the basketball bouncing against the floor.

Suddenly, Derek closed the gap between them. But she quickly pivoted out of his reach.

"And I don't play ball with chicks in skirts. It's too..." He shook his head and swallowed hard. "Distracting."

She grinned. "You mean, it's too easy to lose!"

"Me lose to a girl?" He put his hands on his hips and his sonorous laugh echoed throughout the court. "Are you kidding me?"

She kept a straight face and dribbled the ball until his laughter finally died away.

"You ever play before?" he asked. The wariness in his voice bolstered her false bravado.

She hesitated for a few seconds, feeling a strong urge to just hand over the ball and walk away from him, from the task she was hired to do. What was she thinking going head-to-head in anything, let alone basketball, with one of the NBA's top forwards?

She huffed out a breath. "I think you know the answer to that," she chided.

He raised a brow, flexed his fingers. "You got one shot off me, you won't get another."

"We'll see about that," she countered, although by the look on his face, she knew he was telling the truth. He wasn't going to go easy on her.

"Half court press," she said, circling around him. "First one to hit five baskets wins."

He clapped his hands together, as if he'd already won. "Game on! You might as well start packing up that Gucci bag and crying for your mama."

My what? she thought, and before she knew what was happening, Derek smacked the ball out of her hand. A few seconds later he made a humongous, swinging-on-the-edge-of-the-net dunk and landed on both feet. Grabbing the ball, he passed it to her as she caught up to meet him.

Her bare feet pounded the floor as she rounded him and then faked him out for a not-so-easy layup.

"One–one. Nice job," he commented.

The ball bounced once on the floor and Derek grabbed it. She edged toward him until they were practically toe-to-toe and attempted to steal the ball, but he held it high over his head.

"No traveling!" she shouted, reaching for it, knowing there was no way she could grab it. At five feet six inches, she was clearly outmatched. But she kept stretching for it anyway and felt her shirt pull out from the waistband of her skirt. But she didn't care. Now was not the time for fashion.

She had to win.

If not for him, for herself. To prove that she could compete again and not run away or give up.

He faked her out and dribbled toward the three-point line, where he immediately shot the ball. Natalie watched it arc over her head and drop through the net without kicking up a breeze, which would have been welcome in the hot air.

Derek cupped his hands around his mouth. "He shoots! He scores!" he shouted.

"Don't rub it in," she complained as she trotted over to pick up the ball. "Didn't your mother tell you that was bad sportsmanship?"

"She never had to," he answered.

She dribbled the ball downcourt.

"Why is that?" she called back to him.

His sneakers screeched to a halt as he caught up to her.

"Because I never lost," he replied with a toothy grin.

She shot him a hard pass. "You're impossible!"

"And you're losing," he taunted, and then groaned when she immediately stole the ball again.

She pivoted just under the basket. "Not for long," she said, and sprung for the layup. But it was nothing but rim, and the ball ended back in Derek's palms.

"You were saying?" he teased. She scowled and stuck out her tongue at him.

Derek broke the tension with some fancy footwork and dribbling á la Harlem Globetrotters that left her doubled over with laughter. He was so charming and playful that she almost forgot she was supposed to be competing against him—a dangerous combination.

In the middle of his antics, she saw an opportunity to smack the ball out of his hands and she did.

Changing direction, she sprinted back toward the basket and grit out a mental prayer. "Please let this one go in, please let this one go in." She was amazed when the ball sailed through, barely moving the net.

"I'm impressed," said Derek, grabbing the ball after the first bounce. "Luck is definitely with the lady tonight. It's all tied up now and it's anyone's game. You ready?"

Beads of sweat tickled the base of her spine. "I'm always ready," she huffed delicately, trying to catch her breath.

He circled around her, dribbling the ball, slow and easy. "Well. Just so you think you're not just another pretty face who thinks she's got game…"

He passed her the ball, moved behind her and put his arm around her waist.

"Let's see how you play defense," he challenged.

Derek's powerful body moved with hers in a heated battle for possession of the ball. She bit her lip against the desire that stole her breath away.

Inhaling deeply, she bent her legs to gain more traction, but his iron-hard thighs swished against her backside, throwing her off balance, and she struggled to maintain control of the ball and her senses. Finally she broke away and went east–west, weaving around him.

A second later his hands caught her around the waist and he vaulted her up toward the basket. She slammed the ball into the net, and the next thing she knew her feet were on the ground, and her heart was in her throat.

He spun her around to face him, but he didn't let go of her.

"You win."

His voice, low and sweet, tented a cloak of intimacy around them, as if she'd just conquered him in the bedroom rather than on the basketball court.

She gulped back a cry of indignation under his mesmerizing gaze. "B-but you helped me make the basket," she protested.

His gray eyes lit up with an I-play-for-keeps kind of fire.

"We all need a lift now and then. Don't you agree?"

Natalie nodded, still a little shocked at how comfortable she'd felt in Derek's arms. He was her client, so officially he was off-limits. That was a good thing.

She never let her heart get in the way of her profession, and she wouldn't start now.

She met his eyes, hoping he couldn't see the desire that remained in her own. "Um. The game is over. You can let me go now."

He dropped his hands, reluctantly it seemed, and led her to a row of courtside seats.

"How'd you learn to play ball like that?" he said, tossing her a towel before grabbing one for himself.

She caught it with one hand. "Thanks. It's a long story," she murmured and sat, her heart racing.

He wiped the sweat from his face. "I'd like to hear it sometime."

The smile on his full lips invited her fantasies, and she tried not to stare at his wet, glistening body, so deep and dark with angles and planes. He was all muscle and bone and length.

She knew she could spend a night, or better yet, a lifetime exploring and never satiate her need to discover him. With effort, she tore her eyes away and checked her watch.

"I don't think that would be a good idea."

Derek turned and spread his arms wide. "Why not? Look at me, I'm an open book."

Her face warmed under his watchful eyes, beckoning her lips to smile in response. She longed to talk to someone about other things besides goal-setting and efficient and organized living.

She had a few close girlfriends, but she rarely confided in them. Since she was a life coach and a former psychologist, they naturally expected her to have all the answers to life's toughest questions. They didn't realize that she struggled to make sense of things, too.

While Derek seemed sincere, she couldn't allow herself to get hurt. Although she'd taken a huge risk and played an innocent game of basketball with him, her heart and her bed were out of bounds.

"I doubt that," Natalie said. She walked back over to the place where she'd left her stuff lying in a heap.

Derek followed her and she felt his eyes on her as she bent to zip up her stiletto boots, ignoring the outstretched arm he offered to help her balance. She slipped on her now-wrinkled suit coat and dropped her panty hose into her purse.

He touched her arm, leaving it pulsating with heat in the wake of his touch. "But what about the rules of engagement?"

Her heart raced anew and she was unnerved that he'd remembered, let alone repeated, something she'd said earlier.

She clutched at her belongings, glad to have something to hold on to. "I'll meet you at your house at 8:00 a.m. sharp tomorrow."

He nodded. "It's a date."

She didn't respond. Unconsciously she just wanted to savor the sound of his voice, tantalizing her imagination, hinting at promise and pleasure. In his eyes, she saw unmitigated need and unyielding desire.

As she turned and walked off the practice court, only one thing was on her mind. Could he possibly feel thosc cmotions for her? Or had she only seen herself reflected in his gray eyes?

Chapter 2

The next morning, the taxi taking Natalie to Derek's Brooklyn apartment snaked through rush-hour traffic. Frustrated drivers honked horns and shouted out car windows. Yet she was so focused on the task before her that she barely heard any of it.

Although her initial research was complete and all of the necessary arrangements had been made, being efficient didn't erase the knots in her stomach. Convincing Derek to go along with her plan wouldn't be easy, but she knew it was the only way to help him get his life back on track.

When they finally arrived, her mouth fell open. Derek was sitting on the front stoop reading a newspaper. Waiting for her.

She paid her fare, stepped out of the taxi and

slammed the door, half wishing she could jump back in and go home.

He looked up and folded the paper. "You're late," he chided.

His eyes tumbled over her body and her face flushed hot with embarrassment. She was never late for a client meeting or anything else for that matter.

She gulped in a breath. "I'm sorry. Will you forgive me?"

He crossed his arms on his knees, a slight smile upon his lips. "That depends on the excuse."

She hesitated. The "I got caught in traffic" line wouldn't fly, especially since she was supposed to be a pro at managing time. But she couldn't tell him the entire truth, either.

How she'd tossed and turned all night, remembering the feel of his massive body brushing against hers during their playful game of one-on-one. The sensual instant replay had eventually lulled her to sleep.

Yet when she'd woken up, bleary-eyed and aroused, she'd almost called Derek's manager to tell him to find someone else. All because of a six-letter word that starts with *D* and ends with heartbreak:

Desire.

Muscles, hard and lean, twisted out of his sleeves. His eyes caught her looking and his smile widened.

"Well?"

Her face heated again. *Keep your mind on the mission, not on his body.*

"I overslept," she blurted. That was the truth, although she still couldn't quite believe it herself. She never slept late, not even on holidays. There was nothing, or no one, to keep her in bed past 5:00 a.m.

Derek tossed the paper aside. "I'm not surprised."

"Excuse me?" she said, trying not to sound offended.

He leaned back on one elbow. "Playing basketball in bare feet had to be tough."

His eyes rambled over her shoulders, down her turquoise sundress and settled on her legs.

He whistled low. "But, girl, you've definitely got game."

The exposed areas of her skin tingled as she stared at him with a mix of pleasure and astonishment.

Derek had every right to be angry, especially after her little speech about time management and organization. Yet he was clearly flirting with her.

Why?

More troubling was the fact that she enjoyed it—a dangerous way to feel. She decided it was best to ignore his comment, and her growing attraction to him.

"Nevertheless, it's unacceptable and—"

"Unpredictable." He cut her off and flashed a brilliant smile. "I like it."

She choked back a laugh. As someone who alphabetized every spice and canned good in her kitchen, she was the least unpredictable person on the planet. It was just another indication that he wasn't her type. Not that she cared, she reminded herself.

"Just do me a favor," he continued. "The next time you're going to be late, at least give me a call."

He was right. "I'm sorry," she admitted. "But I just

assumed you'd be sleeping and that I'd have to get *you* out of bed when I got here."

He chuckled and held up his hands. "Whoa, not on the first date!"

She blew out a breath and put her hands on her hips. "Mr. Lansing, this is not a date, and quite frankly, I don't think I need to remind you why I'm here."

Derek's amused expression turned grim. "You're right."

He tucked the newspaper under his arm, stood and opened the door.

She stepped inside and he led her to a freight elevator that had a huge basketball with the number seventeen painted on it.

"A housewarming gift from my neighbor," he said, punching in a code. His voice suddenly dropped to a whisper. "He's an artist. I guess he thought I'd forget my own number."

She stifled a laugh as the doors opened with a monstrous squeal. After they were both inside, Derek slid the heavy metal gate closed with ease.

The elevator began its slow, creaky ascent. Silence stretched between them. Yet something crackled, too.

Neither understood nor acknowledged it, but it was still there, manifested in the way he leaned against the wall, inviting her eyes to take in the length of his legs and her hands to take hold of the brute strength she knew lay beneath the loose-fitting navy-blue athletic pants. It dared her nose to inhale deeply the hint of spicy cologne in the air, knowing it would make her hunger even more for the man who wore it.

Time stood still. Suspended by that delicious bubble of heat neither hoped would break.

Suddenly the elevator lurched to a stop and Natalie lost her balance. She grabbed hold of Derek's outstretched hand and he pulled her into his arms where she landed with her cheek nestled against the tight fabric of his T-shirt. In his tight embrace, her heart flipped so loudly in her chest she was sure he could hear and feel it.

"This elevator has a mind of its own," he explained. "I should have warned you. Are you okay?"

She looked up, touched by the concern in his gray eyes. "Yes, I'm just a little startled, that's all."

He nodded. "Still, it needs to be fixed." His full lips parted into a warm smile. "But today I'm kind of glad it wasn't."

Was it her imagination or did his embrace get even tighter?

He seemed to be waiting for her to respond and she wanted to say, "Me, too," but she remained silent. Yet there was no mistaking the rush of disappointment she felt when he released her and pulled open the gate.

He bowed slightly and Natalie giggled. "Come on in. I'll make it up to you with a cup of my famous café au lait."

"Ooh-la-la," she joked, her footsteps echoing on the shiny hardwood floor as she followed him.

His converted warehouse apartment was immense. Floor-to-ceiling windows spanned one side of the room, bathing it in gorgeous sunlight. The furniture consisted of a huge flat-screen television, a large leather sectional, a couple of end tables and some modern lamps that, due to all the natural light, probably only got used at night or on rainy days.

Derek tossed the paper onto the sparkling granite countertop and pulled out a high-backed chair.

"Have a seat."

She slipped her purse strap around the back. "Thanks." Derek remained by her side until she was seated, which she thought was a nice gesture. Yet, when he moved to the other side of the counter, she was oddly relieved. Being in his arms those few minutes had spurned a mini whirlpool of desire within her and she knew that she couldn't do anything about it.

She watched him prepare the coffee to distract herself. As he poured the milk into the steamer, his movements were unhurried, graceful, and she began to relax.

It was almost as though he was taking care of her because he felt a need to, rather than simply being hospitable. The feeling was comfortable and she leaned back and exhaled lightly, wondering what it would be like to sit here with him every morning, watching him making coffee, after a night of lovemaking.

His eye caught hers and he winked. It was almost as if he could read her mind and a blush spread over her cheeks.

Natalie glanced around. "Your apartment is nice." She hesitated. "Did you just move in?"

Derek shook his head, his voice slightly raised over the sounds of the coffee machine. "No, I've been living here since I signed with the Skylarks three years ago."

He poured two mugs of coffee, then topped both off

with the steamed milk. When he set one mug down, her nostrils twitched as she lightly inhaled the rich aroma.

"With all the traveling we do during the season," Derek continued, "I'm just not around that much."

His shoulders rolled back, as if he was trying to loosen some imaginary knots, but the subtle hitch in the tone of his voice was real. She had to explore it, if only to guide him to a place where he could begin to trust her.

"Being on the road so much must be hard. My clients complain about that all the time," she said, empathizing. "This place is huge. Maybe it needs some more furniture or something. So it won't feel so…um…empty when you come home."

Derek furrowed his brow and looked past her into the living room. "It doesn't look empty to me. I've got my top-of-the-line TV, a custom-built couch and the remote." His eyes settled back on hers. "What more could a man want after a long trip?"

She shrugged and slid her mug closer, debating whether to take another sip under his gaze. It was watchful, curious and just plain sexy. Yet he seemed totally unaware of her at the moment and instead appeared to be pondering her question seriously.

Suddenly, Derek picked up both coffee mugs and put them aside. "But in a way, though, I think you may be right." He leaned both elbows on the counter. "This place *is* missing something."

Derek inched closer, his head and eyes nearly parallel now with hers. Natalie held her breath, trying not to focus on his full lips and strong jaw threatening her ability to remain aloof.

"It needs a woman's touch," he teased. "Interested?"

His steel-gray eyes had a hint of fire in them. But there was no question that the rest of him, from his locks down to his toes, was smoking hot.

Interested? She'd be a fool not to be, and an even bigger fool to fall for his charm and good looks.

This is business, she reminded herself as she picked up her mug and leveled her eyes at him.

Steam from the hot liquid rose between them, tickling her nose. Her lower abdomen pulsed with the tension of desire.

Derek didn't move. Neither did Natalie.

She swallowed hard. His eyes immediately flicked down to trace the curve of her neck and her throat went dry. She'd always had a hate/curse relationship with her long neck, but the way Derek was looking at it made her wish it was even longer.

Although she was flattered by his interest, the man was making her feel things that could only hurt her in the end.

"I'm not available," she said, her voice flat.

And she wasn't. To any man.

Getting her heart broken was not on her to-do list.

His arms squeaked against the counter like fingernails scratching down a chalkboard as he stood. His back was ramrod-straight and he didn't say a word. It was clear she'd hurt him and that surprised her. She knew his reputation. It wasn't as if he didn't have other options for female companionship. It shouldn't even matter that she'd rejected him.

Then why did she get the sense that it did?

Time to change the subject.

She took another sip of the coffee.

"Ooh-la-la is right. This is heavenly." She sighed. "By far the best café au lait I've ever tasted."

The smile returned to his face, although her heart was heavy with the knowledge that when he heard what she was about to say, it wouldn't last long.

"I thought you'd like it," he responded. "Now that I've been benched for the next few days, I've got a lot of time on my hands."

He rubbed his palms together as if he were formulating a devious plan. "So what's on the agenda first? I've got a mountain of basketball shoes sitting in the middle of my closet just dying to be organized. One of the reasons I think I'm late in the morning is because I can never find shoes that match."

She flipped open her notebook. "That's not quite what I had in mind."

He frowned as he stirred some sugar into his coffee. "O-kay. Maybe we can go shopping for a couple of new alarm clocks that have really annoying rings. The one on my phone obviously isn't enough to wake me up."

She crossed her legs to steady her nerves, aware of his eyes on them as he sipped his coffee.

"Actually, we're going to see your father."

Derek clattered his mug against the granite countertop. "What are you talking about?"

Her heart lurched at the sudden change in his demeanor. The hard stare he gave her now was a far cry from the way he'd been looking at her moments earlier.

She shifted in her seat. "I'm talking about making things right with your family, especially your dad."

He flattened his palms on the counter.

"How did you find out about him?" he demanded. "I thought you were a life coach, not a private detective."

She kept her voice calm. "I do background research on all my clients, and it's amazing what you can find archived on the internet. The newspaper articles are all there and—"

He cut her off with a wave of his hand. "My dad doesn't want anything to do with me. Trust me."

"I think the opposite is true," she ventured.

His eyes narrowed. "What do you mean?"

"I don't think you want anything to do with *him*."

He said nothing, yet something seemed to deflate within him.

"As I was saying, there are tons of articles about your rags-to-riches success story on the web, but your family is rarely mentioned."

"So?" he challenged. "I thought you were here to help me get off the bench and back on the basketball court where I belong, not poke around where you don't belong."

She understood his anger, but she wasn't going to let herself be deterred by it.

"I'm here to help you in any way I can," she replied.

Derek walked around the counter, sat on the chair opposite her and crossed his arms. "Well, you can start by leaving my past out of it."

She shook her head. "I'm sorry. I can't do that."

He leaned forward. "Why not?"

She met his eyes and kept her voice firm. "Sometimes when people have unresolved issues in their past, it can affect their lives in the present, as well as the future. No matter how successful they become, there's always something missing."

She knew that feeling all too well. It was something she struggled with every day.

He waved her comment away and crossed his arms over his massive chest. "That sounds like some kind of self-help mumbo jumbo, *Dr. Kenyon.*"

She took in a sharp breath and brought her hand to her mouth.

"Don't look so shocked that I did a little investigation of my own," he advised.

She said nothing for a moment, preferring to forget about that part of her life. A time when she'd tried to start over, and failed miserably.

"Actually, I'm glad to hear that you did a little digging on your own," she said, recovering quickly. "It shows you're highly invested in doing things in your life differently."

"Or it could show that I'm highly interested in you," he added, watching her for her reaction.

Her heart fluttered, yet she managed to keep her expression calm and her voice light. "I'd heard you were a huge flirt, Derek. You don't have to prove it to me."

His brows knit together and she sensed he was disappointed with her response. What had he expected her to say? Her interest in him was strictly professional and her fantasies were hers alone.

"Do you remember Jamal Carter?" The former NBA star turned heroin addict had been her last patient in her short-lived second career as a psychologist.

Her insides quaked at the memory of their counseling sessions. Some of the stories Jamal had told her about growing up in one of the fiercest projects in Brooklyn still haunted her. Despite his wealth and success, he could never get past all the pain he'd experienced as a child.

She'd quit practicing psychology soon after his death from suicide. Even though she knew it wasn't her fault, not a day went by when she didn't ask herself if she could have done or said something to prevent it. Questions that would forever remain unanswered.

Derek ran a hand through his locks and looked uncomfortable. "Of course I remember him. He grew up in the same projects I did. I was brought in to replace him on the team after he died. You were Jamal's therapist?"

She nodded. "I counseled Jamal for a few months before he died. He was an incredibly gifted and successful athlete. But his past ultimately destroyed him."

He crossed his arms. "That's not going to happen to me," he insisted, looking away.

She hated the prideful tone in his voice, yet she knew it wasn't the result of arrogance. The man was wealthy, yet he didn't flaunt it like some of her other clients. There was something that mattered more to him than money and whatever it was, she had a feeling it scared him more than he wanted to admit.

"Don't you see, Derek? It is already starting to happen!"

He lowered his head, refusing to look at her even when she slid off the chair and stood next to him.

"Your playing has been off-kilter for months, you've been suspended right before the most important games of the season and your reputation in the media has taken a major hit."

"I know," he muttered, running his hand down his face. "I can't seem to get it together. I don't know what's wrong with me."

Natalie smiled inwardly, secretly pleased he didn't deny what was happening to him, even if he didn't know what it was.

On the flip side, it made Derek even more attractive to her. He was less of an untouchable sports celebrity and ultimately more human.

"Do you really think seeing my family is going to help?" He lifted his head. "I haven't spoken to my dad or my brother in over ten years. Not since high school," he murmured. "Can you believe that?"

The shame in his voice curdled in her ear. It was so real and so familiar that she just wanted to bolt. But perhaps it was time for her to stop running. Sometimes her faith and her inner drive to succeed, no matter the consequences, were the only things that kept her going.

She forced her voice steady. "You can do this. I'll help you."

He shook his head again. "No, Natalie." Derek's voice was firm. "I haven't seen them in years. It will never work."

"Only because you won't let it," she charged, even though she knew she should be more patient. The stubborn determination in his eyes upset her because it could only mean one thing: his mind was made up.

She turned away and grabbed her purse. Why couldn't he see that this was for the best? Even worse, why did she care so much? So soon? She had that irrefutable feeling in the pit of her stomach that made her want to dive into his muscular arms and never come up for air.

"Thanks for the coffee," she snapped. For reasons she knew she'd analyze to death later on, she was deeply hurt by his rejection of her plan. "I'll let Tony know that we won't be working together."

Her heels tapped out a brisk rhythm as she walked to the elevator.

As she was searching for the down button, Derek placed one arm against the wall and turned her around to face him. Her breath came out in a rush of surprise.

"There's a security code," he reminded her.

"So why don't you punch it in, so I can leave," she retorted.

He didn't move.

Behind his gray eyes: pure pain.

Between their bodies: pure heat.

"Look. I hurt a lot of people when I was coming up. My family mostly. And you're right. I need someone to walk through this with me." He stepped a little closer. "Someone who doesn't want anything personal from me."

Natalie's heart plummeted and bottomed out in frustration. Mostly at herself for thinking the spark she'd felt between them yesterday and this morning was more than just a bunch of molecules colliding together.

Derek wouldn't be the first person who hadn't bothered to look beneath her expensive clothes and runway-model looks. No one but she knew that she existed within a carefully crafted persona, designed over the years to avoid being hurt by anyone.

She'd given up on the dream to be loved for who she was a long time ago.

Nothing personal, huh?

Fine. She could keep it real. *Real superficial.*

Besides, keeping it casual was just the way she liked all her relationships to be, business or otherwise. She hadn't been called "Ice Queen" back in her skating days for nothing.

She met his eyes and plastered on a confident smile that belied her true feelings. "All I want is to get you back on that court. And that's exactly what I'm going to do."

He ran a thumb along her jawline and she shivered at the gentleness of his touch.

"Is that a promise?"

She had a feeling that despite his imposing presence and competitive spirit, there was a soft and tender side to him that was rarely seen. She was always a sucker for teddy bears, especially a big, hard-muscled one like Derek.

She tilted her head, trying not to lose her professional composure. "You want to play me for it?" she challenged, not realizing that her voice had dropped to a low whisper.

He moved even closer and put his other hand against the wall where she leaned, barely able to breathe. She was trapped, although not unpleasantly, in a dual firestorm of will.

Her nose twitched. Something that sometimes happened when she got nervous or excited. In this unusual situation, she was both.

"So, what's in it for you?"

His question hit her rock-square in the gut. It wasn't the money she'd make, that meant nothing to her. Instead she thought of Jamal, her grandparents and her parents. All gone now. Nothing left for her but memories, dead dreams and wishes for more time.

How does one explain all that?

Yet, for the first time in a long time, she felt hope.

Her eyes met his and her voice was strong. "A chance to see a family come together instead of being torn apart."

Derek punched in the security code and slid the elevator door open. "I'll have a car pick you up this evening."

There it was again. The alluring sound in his voice making her skin tingle in all the places it shouldn't.

But how to resist the rest of him? The hair she longed to twist around her finger, the broad shoulders she wanted to trace, the full lips that looked too delicious not to kiss. She certainly couldn't work with a blindfold on her face.

She nodded, but didn't say anything else as she entered the elevator. When she turned around, their eyes locked and she froze, not in fear, but in anticipation. As she descended to the ground, she hoped she wouldn't pay for digging into his past with her heart.

Chapter 3

Derek felt a sensual hunger unlike any he'd ever known at the sight of Natalie stepping out of the limousine. She could have melted the tar right out of the tarmac as she walked toward him with those long legs and curves that could drive a man crazy and make him lose himself, or worse, his independence.

At age twenty-nine staring down the hard-nosed barrel of thirty, he was rich beyond his wildest dreams playing the game he'd loved ever since he was a young boy growing up in the notorious Pinecrest projects. He'd made it. He'd beaten the system all but designed to shackle him.

Yet the only thing he didn't have was what he wanted most of all: a family, with a woman he could call his own.

Playing pro basketball for most of the year and doing

intense training during the off-season wasn't exactly conducive to a mortgage on a house in the suburbs with a picket fence and a couple of kids, or a commitment to one woman for more than an evening.

His playboy rep in the league was only an excuse for the truth. A real woman, one like Natalie perhaps, wouldn't want more than a night with him anyway, if she knew how he'd treated his own flesh and blood during his rise to the top.

He found himself standing even taller when Natalie finally reached him.

A breeze ruffled her short black hair, shorn into a pixie cut, and he noticed she was shivering, despite the warm evening temperature.

She clamped her hands over her small ears. "Why didn't you tell me we were flying?" she shouted over the noisy din of a plane taking off.

He took one hand away from her ear and leaned in close. Her scent, warm apricots and vanilla, made him wish he could get even closer.

He gestured to the sleek aircraft in front of him and smiled. "Do you like her?"

Although the smile she returned was gracious, her eyes flicked around, seeming to take in every detail of his beloved private plane. Something was bothering her and he needed to find out what it was.

After a few moments, when it was quieter, she jerked her chin at him. "I like *her,* but I'd rather drive."

Was she kidding? Baker's Falls was only an hour away by plane. In his mind, the only way to travel was by plane.

He stepped back with a mock look of chagrin. "Then I guess you don't want the bottle of Dom Pérignon I have on ice."

She pointed to the cap on top of his head. "You know I think they have laws against pilots drinking while flying, or at least they should!" she exclaimed.

He reached for her arm and gave it a gentle squeeze to reassure her.

"Take it easy. I was just kidding. I would never put my passengers in harm's way."

She visibly relaxed, but only a little, and he wondered why she seemed so uptight. Nervous even. Was she regretting the decision to help him?

"But I *will* give you a rain check on that Dom, if you promise not to look at me cross-eyed." He winked.

She frowned and seemed not to hear him.

Since his attempt at comedy to make her feel more at ease was a dismal failure, he decided to try a third alternative: being the perfect gentleman. Not that he wasn't normally. He was just out of practice.

When he'd first started playing professional basketball, he'd tried the booty-call-in-every-state thing. It had been fun for a while and the sex was a welcome release, but the hassle and drama eventually cancelled out any pleasure.

So one day he'd decided to quit the scene—cold-turkey style. Despite the pressure from his teammates, he'd stopped going out after games and instead returned to his apartment or hotel room and watched television.

He'd been flying solo so long he'd forgotten what it was like to put someone else's needs ahead of his own.

Now, his whole future depended on it.

Shame burned in his gut, but he ignored the pain and offered Natalie his hand.

"We're almost ready to take off."

Her fingers, slightly clammy, latched on to his a little tighter than he expected, but he didn't complain. He liked the feel of her small hand in his and a part of him wanted to tug her closer.

He opened the passenger's-side door of the single-engine plane.

"All aboard," he called out, subtly watching her black designer jeans stretch like hands across the curves of her backside as he assisted her inside. The smooth and elegant way she slid into the passenger seat made him instantly hard.

The mundane task of stowing her luggage helped put the pause button on his libido. Afterward, he sat in the pilot's seat and offered her a pair of headphones. When she refused, he put them on and began making the final preparations for takeoff.

He knew every button and dial on the instrument panel. Normally they calmed him, but today he was nervous. He wasn't looking forward to this journey, and deep down he was afraid. He wasn't sure what type of reaction he was going to receive when he returned to Baker's Falls.

Natalie turned her heart-shaped face to his, and he was suddenly lost in her beauty and the memory of how he'd felt earlier that morning.

The moment the elevator doors had closed, a mix of emptiness and wonder had filled his heart. He wasn't so out of touch that he didn't recognize his feelings as loneliness…and lust.

Looking at Natalie now, he realized she could be the perfect antidote for both. She was the kind of woman who could change a man. Make him better than he was before, and that scared him more than anything.

Her eyes narrowed. "Derek, did you hear me? What time will we land?"

"Sorry." He cleared his throat. "We'll be there in about an hour or so."

Back to good old Baker's Falls. The town where he'd made the choice that changed the course of his life forever.

"Seat belt on, please," commanded Derek as he buckled his own. "I'm about to put her in the air."

Natalie held on to the right armrest so tightly Derek could see her veins, while her left hand was balled into a fist. She stared out the window and seemed ready to jump from the plane at any minute.

Yesterday, by stepping out on the court and playing ball with him, Natalie showed a kind of devilish moxie rarely displayed in any of the women he knew.

But right now, she seemed downright terrified.

He switched his headset to mute, so air traffic control wouldn't be able to hear his conversation.

"Natalie, are you okay?"

She didn't answer. He reached over and touched her chin, so she would face him.

"Have you ever flown in one of these before?"

Her lips quivered and her soft brown eyes were glazed with fear.

"No," she whispered. "To tell you the truth, I'm afraid of flying."

Whoa. He pressed his back against the leather seat. He nodded slowly to buy time, unsure of what to say to appease her fears. In all of his travels, he'd never met anyone who was afraid to fly.

He placed his hand over hers. "If it makes you feel any better, I'm a highly trained pilot. I've had my license for over five years now."

She didn't look convinced. "I see. Does the number of years of experience in flying translate the same as the number of years of experience in driving?"

"Not really," he replied. "Pilots have to fly hundreds of hours more than drivers need to drive before they get their license," he explained. "There are also a ton of tests and other stuff you have to do before you can even go up in the air."

He watched her eyes sweep over the complex instrumentation on the plane's dashboard. She seemed overly nervous and he held out his hand to comfort her. His heart squeezed in his chest when she kept her hands in her lap, bound together in a tight fist. A clear refusal of his advances.

"Flying is much safer than driving. You have nothing to worry about."

Her shoulders sagged and it occurred to him that his response was insensitive. Once again, he'd proved he had a knack for saying the wrong thing at precisely the wrong time.

Right now though, as much as he wanted to, he didn't have time to explore her fears. He had to get his plane up in the air before it was grounded and he was fined by the FAA.

"I'm sorry you're afraid," he said, trying again. "I'm afraid of hot tubs and—"

To his surprise, she started to laugh. "Are you serious?"

He nodded, and his body shuddered involuntarily from head to toe with disgust. "Do you know how many germs are in those things?"

Their laughter ebbed away and again he reached for her hand, so small in his own. He ran his thumb over her knuckles, calming her gently in the only way he knew how, as her eyes danced with his at the root of desire.

This time she didn't pull away.

"Ready to touch the sky?"

She nodded, and her smile was braver now, and somehow it managed to make her even more beautiful.

"I'd keep holding your hand, but I think it's better to keep both hands on the steering wheel."

He forced himself to look away from Natalie and switched his microphone live. After a few instructions from air traffic control, he started to taxi the plane down the runway, his brow furrowed with concentration.

Outside the cockpit, the world blurred and his heart quickened in wild anticipation as the plane sped faster and faster until the nose lifted into the twilight and everything around them fell away.

He broke out in a light sweat, exhilarated by the rush that fueled what some considered a crazy hobby. Being up in the air was one of his favorite places to be. With Natalie at his side, it felt more right than ever before.

When it was safe to do so, he glanced over at her. Eyes tightly shut, her hands gripped the armrests, the crescent of her breasts hidden under her lace-trimmed tunic. He pressed his lips together. Something deeper and more potent than simple concern washed over him.

For a moment he imagined her eyes were shut due to overwhelming pleasure, not fear. The urgent feel of her hands anchored to him as his tongue traveled across the silk of her skin in the ultimate road trip.

"Open your eyes, Natalie," he coaxed, his voice low with a need he knew was just beginning. "You're missing the view."

Her eyes flickered open and she stared ahead open-mouthed. Wide stripes of burnished orange laced with muted pink encircled them. She dropped her hands from the armrests.

"Oh, Derek, it's breathtaking!" she exclaimed. "I never thought flying could be this beautiful."

I think she's going to be okay.

His heart soared with joy and relief as he watched her gaze out the window.

She turned to him, her eyes shining with delight. "Is this why you like to fly?"

His eyes moved across her tawny-brown skin, the color of fall acorns, glowing in the radiance of the sunset.

"I get to touch heaven," he replied, nodding. "There's nothing else like it."

He didn't bother mentioning the other reasons.

Up here he was away from the constant pressure to perform and the daily stress of maintaining his lifestyle. The sky was like a blank slate and he imagined that all his past mistakes were erased, or at least hidden among the clouds.

Until wheels touched ground and the cold reality hit hard.

Nothing about his life had changed.

She wouldn't understand anyway.

The woman who made it her business to run other people's lives probably ran her own with clocklike precision. On the other hand, he'd had no trouble making a mess out of his own.

Still he pushed aside the anguish that dogged his conscience, refusing to entertain any more doubts. This time, when he landed, things *would* be different. Not right away, he realized, but soon.

Natalie fluffed her hair. "I can imagine flying must be an expensive hobby."

Her practical tone reminded him of his accountant. He'd warned Derek not to buy the plane, citing ongoing maintenance, fuel, storage and security costs, but he did it anyway.

"It is," he admitted, trying not to sound defensive. "But you know every man has to have a few toys."

As the words flew out of his mouth he realized how immature they sounded. He was living a life many dreamed of, but few achieved, yet what did he have to really show for it? Who did he have to share it all with?

"Where'd you grow up?" he asked.

Her voice was shy. "You're not going to believe this," she replied. "Park Avenue."

"Really?"

She nodded. "My parents were both surgeons at Lenox Hill Hospital, and they were the first African-Americans to purchase an apartment in our co-op," she said, her face beaming with pride.

"Well, my parents were one of the first to move out of Pinecrest. My brother Wes, my dad and I moved to Baker's Falls at the beginning of my freshman year in high school."

He paused a moment, waiting for her to ask about his mother, but she didn't. He breathed a sigh of relief.

"So I guess we do have something in common."

"What's that?" she asked.

"Parents who cared enough to take a risk for the sake of their kids."

She turned away, seeming to fold inside herself, and was quiet. Just like that, the easy camaraderie they'd shared was gone and he knew he'd said something wrong again.

He rubbed a hand down his face and swore inwardly. Flying a plane was so much easier than understanding a woman.

Suddenly there was a loss of elevation.

Natalie screamed and clutched the armrests. "What was that?"

The sound raked his ears and he gritted his teeth. "Air pocket," he explained. "Nothing to worry about."

"Tell that to my stomach," she moaned, pointing to it.

He glanced at her quickly, and her eyes were lidded as she leaned her head against the tiny window.

Oh, man. He thought dealing with a fear of flying was bad, but a nauseated woman was much, much worse. If he was ever lucky enough to get married, he'd be a blubbering idiot when his wife got pregnant and started running to the bathroom every morning.

The image terrified him. He cleared his throat. "Barf bags are under the seat."

She clucked her tongue at him. "Gross! I would never do that in front of a guy," she insisted, her face ashen. "No matter how sick I felt."

He breathed out a slow sigh of relief. "I'm glad to hear it, but I thought I'd inform you, just to be on the safe side."

"Thanks," she replied. "But I won't be needing them."

Derek scanned the instrumentation panel and spoke with air traffic control, who informed him that the winds had shifted from south to northwest.

They bumped along for a few more minutes as Derek struggled to keep the plane steady and his image intact. He'd made it his mission in life to avoid showing weakness to anyone—his opponents, his teammates, but especially women.

He winced when Natalie squealed with fright so loudly the sound bounced off every surface of the cockpit.

"Are you sure you know how to fly this thing?" she screamed.

"Don't worry," he soothed, keeping his eyes on the horizon and wishing he could kiss her fears away instead. "I'll take care of you. I promise."

Just then, the ride smoothed out and he blew out a breath. He turned to Natalie and gave her a triumphant smile.

"You see? Nothing to worry about. My father taught me to never break a promise. I can't let anything happen to all that beauty."

A smile feathered across Natalie's face, and Derek was thankful she took his compliment in stride. He figured that with her looks, she'd probably heard it all. A beautiful woman like her had to have a boyfriend.

Even so, she seemed like the type of woman who chose her man the way she did her diamonds—wisely and with much examination. Would he ever make the cut? Did he even want to?

Natalie crossed her arms and gave him a questioning look, as if she were trying to figure out if he really meant what he'd said and why.

"I'll feel better when my feet are on solid ground."

"I understand," he said with a nod. He glanced over at her to make sure her seat belt was still fastened. "I'm in the process of making our descent now."

The plane broke through the clouds. The landscape below was laid out like a patchwork quilt. Green countryside and open fields gave way to suburbia and strip malls.

"Touchdown," he muttered as he made a perfect landing, likely the most important one in his life.

When the plane rolled to a stop, Natalie leaned over and pecked him on the cheek. Her soft lips were kindle for the fire he was starting to feel for her, and he resisted the urge to pull her onto his lap. He couldn't remember the last time he was this hard. The woman was kicking it in all the right places.

He remembered how her breasts had moved as she'd

tried to hustle him when they'd played ball. The beads of sweat on her forehead and in the small place at the base of her neck. Lifting her up to make that basket was like grasping a cloud that had a tornado at its root. She was soft and supple on the outside. Undeniably wild at the core.

He wanted to know more about her. And over the next few days she would get to know him—the real Derek. Not the guy who'd won MVP his first year in the NBA. Not the guy they loved to trash-talk on ESPN SportsCenter. Not the guy who became a millionaire several times over at age eighteen.

When this was all over, would she still look at him the same way she was now?

"Thank you for getting us here safely. I can see now that you are a man of your word."

She had no way of knowing that the opposite was true.

He'd betrayed them all. His dad, his brother and, most of all, himself. All for the glory of the game.

And look where it got you, he thought.

Basketball was supposed to be his ticket to happiness, not to regret. He felt in his heart that God had given him a gift, a talent, but somehow on his way to greatness, he'd lost sight of his true purpose.

Natalie's voice broke through his thoughts. "By the way, I booked a room at a cute bed-and-breakfast."

She cleared her throat and seemed embarrassed. "I looked for other accommodations, but it was the only place to stay in town and I figured that would be best. Are you familiar with it?"

His stomach lurched, and for a moment he thought he was going to be sick. He was afraid she'd book that place. He needed more time!

"Derek, are you okay?"

He looked into her warm eyes, at the goodness he saw there, and he realized that only when he made peace with the past, could he even possibly think about a future…with anyone.

It was time to grow up and be the man he was created to be.

He forced a smile. "Yeah. Let's do this."

He opened the door and disembarked the plane. Fear ratcheted through his body and lodged there like an unwelcome guest. There was no turning back now. He was about to come face-to-face with the first person from his past—his brother.

Chapter 4

About twenty minutes later Derek slowed the car to a stop. Natalie sucked in a breath at the sight of the huge Victorian house that was to be their dwelling for the next few days.

Although it was nearly dark outside, she could see that the Belle Amour Bed & Breakfast was as beautiful as its name. The Queen Anne–style mansion had overhanging eaves, leaded windows, a wraparound porch and, to Natalie's delight, a round, dome-shaped tower.

She shivered with anticipation, eager to help Derek restore his relationship with his family. Hopefully, this trip would be the start of a brand-new beginning.

Perhaps for both of us.

Although it saddened her that a relationship with him was out of the question, in the back of her mind, she hoped that he would think of her as more than his life coach. If anything else, she hoped they could at least be friends.

Derek cut the engine. "Home, sweet home," he said quietly.

Her eyes widened. "You grew up here?"

He draped his arm over the steering wheel, tension lining his face, and stared past her.

"Yeah, but it wasn't a B and B when we moved here. It was a dump."

Natalie glanced back at the house and could hardly believe what he was saying.

"The structure was sound, but inside, the place was a wreck. It stood empty for years. My pops was crazy enough to buy it. He spent years fixing it up."

The frown on his face was wistful and sad. "My brother and his wife own it now."

Natalie was curious about Derek's change in mood. Had he had the opportunity to purchase the home at one time? Derek didn't seem like the white-picket-fence-and-vegetable-garden type of man. Or was there something else he regretted?

The psychologist in her wanted to know the inner workings of this man. But she knew that if she was lying in bed alone and thinking about him touching her, professionalism would be totally forgotten.

Warmth flooded her inner thighs and she squeezed them together to try to quell the pleasurable sensation, but the movement only enhanced it.

"I know you were a freshman in high school, but

what age were you when you moved to Baker's Falls?" she asked in what she hoped was a steady voice.

He leaned back against the leather seat. "I was thirteen. Wes, my brother, was ten. My dad told us we were leaving Pinecrest and moving up in the world. Just like *The Jeffersons.*"

Derek fingered one shoulder-length dreadlock, his expression sober.

"But when we got here," he continued, "it seemed like nothing had changed except the zip code. Even the rats were the same."

Natalie shuddered. "Rats?"

He nodded. His voice grave, adding, "Big as cats!"

She peered at the house again, disgust slithering through her body.

Derek chuckled. "I'm sure they're gone by now." He patted her shoulder. "Don't worry."

His polite touch translated into a slingshot of pleasure. It arrowed through her, making her want to close her eyes and indulge in its power, yet somehow she managed to keep her eyes on his face.

"Then let's not wait a moment longer, let's go!"

She moved to open the door, but stopped when he gripped her arm, not tightly, but firmly.

"Wait," he commanded in an urgent tone.

She pulled her arm toward her and he released it. His face was apologetic, and she knew he hadn't meant to grab her so suddenly. He'd acted out of instinct or some kind of need.

"What's wrong?" she asked.

Orangish light from the street lamps filtered through

the leaves, casting shadows inside the car. Yet nothing could hide the flicker of fear she saw in his eyes.

His upper lip trembled slightly. "Do they know I'm coming?"

"Of course not," she assured him gently. "When I booked the reservations yesterday, I put them under my name. You being here will be a complete surprise."

Derek ran his hand over his head and blew out a ragged breath. "God, I don't even remember if my dad or my brother even *like* surprises."

She moved to open the door. "Who doesn't like surprises?" she joked, but she knew Derek wasn't laughing.

He tugged on her arm. "Natalie, I don't know about this."

His touch was sweeter and gentler this time, and she didn't immediately pull away.

"The memories," he continued, releasing her arm. "The things I did… The stuff I said…" He hung his head and his voice drifted off on a trail of pain.

Her heart twisted in her chest with recognition. The way he was feeling right now was how she felt every day. The regret was like a parasite that grew and festered.

She'd hurt her family, too, but it was too late to reconcile.

She inhaled the sweet fragrance of daffodils permeating the air through the open windows of the Jeep and tried to relax. A car suddenly sped past and broke the uncomfortable silence.

Derek lifted his head and turned toward her. "To be

honest, I'm not sure I'm even welcome there anymore," he admitted. "What if they slam the door in my face?"

Natalie had no way of knowing how receptive his brother and father would be to a reunion. His fears could be justified. But as his life coach, it was her job to support and comfort him through it. Without getting emotionally involved, of course. That would be the tough part.

"Reunions are…stressful," Natalie said. "Especially when there are unresolved issues. But family always forgives."

He shook his head. "No way. Not my family," he retorted. "Especially not my dad."

His tone had an edge of bitterness, but she knew it was only because he was hurting inside. And although she hated to see Derek in pain, it meant he could still feel. His heart was still soft. Pliable. And there was still a chance it could heal.

"Maybe he doesn't know how," she said softly. "Maybe it's up to you to show him."

He slumped in his seat and turned his head toward her.

"Why do I feel like I'm about to jump out of a plane?"

She stared at him in amazement. Unknowingly, he'd tapped into something she'd been trying to deny for months.

Deep down, she knew they were both standing on the precipice of some kind of change. Embracing it meant taking a leap of faith, which was hard when you didn't know what was going to happen when you hit the ground.

"Well, I've never jumped out of a plane, but I imagine it's not so bad if you have a parachute." She touched his hand. "And a partner."

He raised a brow, leaned over and ran his finger down her cheek.

"Oh, yeah? Which one are you?"

Her breath hitched. She was grateful he couldn't see the confusion in her eyes. The truth was, she didn't know the answer, and that was the most frightening thing of all.

Leap of faith.

Natalie tilted her head and grinned. "Jump and find out," she dared.

Before he could respond, she grabbed her purse and hopped out of the car. She exhaled in relief when he got out, too.

He pulled their luggage out of the back. "Is that another challenge?"

Natalie lifted the handle of her roll-on suitcase. "You bet it is."

Her heels clicked on the stone pavement as she walked away. Moments later she felt a tug on her elbow.

Derek stepped in close. "Then I accept."

Even darkness couldn't mask the desire that stretched between them. She bit her lip to keep from trembling.

Without another word, he released her, walked onto the porch and set his bags down.

She followed and for a moment she admired Derek under the glow of the porch light. He was the type of guy who always looked fine, no matter what time of day.

Natalie felt a little like Dorothy in *The Wizard of Oz,*

staring at the polished oak door in front of them. What happened when it opened would set the tone for the rest of their time in Baker's Falls.

"Ready?" she asked.

"Almost," he responded.

Her eyes followed his hand as he smoothed the travel wrinkles from the front of his khaki pants. Her mouth went dry as thoughts she shouldn't be having skipped through her brain.

Their eyes met. Although she didn't know exactly what he was feeling at that moment, she imagined it was probably similar to how she'd felt when she was about to skate a championship. Where everything was on the line. Just before she set blade to ice.

He nodded. "Go for it."

Without hesitation, she pressed the bell. Seconds later the door opened with such gusto that the pretty wreath hanging on it nearly fell off its hook.

A man she assumed was Derek's brother, Wes, stood in front of them.

"May I—?"

Natalie held her breath as the expression on the man's face quickly morphed from welcoming to shock and confusion. When he finally released the doorknob, she saw tears in his eyes as he stuck out his hand.

"Aw, what the devil am I doing?" he exclaimed, immediately wrapping Derek in a huge bear hug. "Welcome home, bro!"

The men embraced. What Derek had in height, Wes had in sheer mass.

Wes punched Derek in the shoulder. They laughed, put their fists up and pretended to box each other.

"Man, it's good to see you in person and not just on ESPN."

"I missed you, too, bro," Derek said.

His voice cracked with emotion, but Natalie heard a sense of freedom in it that she hadn't heard before.

Natalie wiped tears from her eyes at the sight of the two brothers, once estranged, now reunited. All because one took a step and the other didn't retreat. She was so happy she felt like cheering. They didn't seem to even notice she was there and that was fine by her.

The two men hugged again.

"We've got a lot of catching up to do," Derek said.

Wes guffawed and slapped Derek's back. "We can't do it here on the porch. This is Baker's Falls. People will talk. C'mon in, man."

The men started to walk inside the house.

Natalie cleared her throat loudly and they turned around.

"Who's this pretty lady?" Wes elbowed Derek. "Don't tell me you forgot the manners Momma taught us."

Although Wes's rebuke was good-natured, Natalie detected a veil of anguish on Derek's face, but it quickly disappeared.

She smiled. "I'm Natalie Kenyon. I believe we spoke earlier on the phone."

"Ah... Yes. I remember now." Wes shook a finger at her. "But you neglected to mention you had my brother in tow."

She waved her palms like jazz hands and her smile was as big as opening night.

"Surprise!"

Their laughter burbled out into the warm spring night, as if they were three old friends rather than three people trying to make the best out of an uncomfortable situation. And for the first time Natalie felt a real sense of hope that Derek and his family could reconcile, even though they still had a long way to go.

"Wes, what's all the commotion out there?"

The laughter died away at the sound of a woman's friendly but stern voice.

Wes took his wife's hand in his. "Janet, I'd like you to meet my brother, Derek Lansing."

Janet's eyes widened as she shook Derek's outstretched hand. "It's great to finally meet you. I've heard so much about you!"

Derek tilted his head toward Wes. "I can only imagine what Wes has told you about me."

Wes slapped him on the back. "All good things, my long-lost brother. All good things," he assured him. "And this is Derek's girlfriend, Natalie."

Natalie's eyes went to Derek's face and he winked at her as though they shared a secret. Heat rose in her face and she opened her mouth to correct Wes. But when she saw Derek give a barely imperceptible shake of his head, she thought better of it.

What was he up to now? she wondered, and decided she'd have to tell his brother the truth at another time. This was a business relationship, not a personal one.

And that's the way it must remain, she told herself.

She shook Janet's hand. "Great to meet you."

"Likewise," Janet said. "We've been holding dinner for you. Are you guys hungry?"

"Starved!" Derek and Natalie proclaimed in unison. They looked at each other and burst out laughing.

"Then let's eat!" Wes said, clapping his hands together in anticipation.

His wife poked his ample stomach. "You've already had your dinner," she reminded him.

"Then this will be my bedtime snack," Wes quipped.

Janet let out a sigh of mock disgust and walked into the house.

Derek grabbed the luggage and strode into the center hall, while Natalie followed. When they were all inside, Wes closed and locked the door.

Derek looked around at the antiques, flea-market knickknacks and dark crown molding. His face held a mix of awe and amusement. "Wow, this place looks different then I remembered it."

Natalie held back a giggle. It was obvious he'd never been in a romantic bed-and-breakfast.

Wes gestured toward the rose-colored walls. "The structure and floor plan hasn't changed."

Janet interrupted. "And I did all the decorating." She beamed.

"It's beautiful," Natalie affirmed.

"Nothing is as beautiful as my girl," Derek said, looping his arm around Natalie's neck.

She felt her face redden. His casualness both pleased and irked her. Why did he insist upon carrying on this charade?

"Go ahead and leave your bags here," Janet directed. "Wes can bring them upstairs later, after he helps me get dinner on the table. Come on, honey."

After Wes dutifully followed his wife into the kitchen, Derek stowed their luggage next to an antique hall tree and began to walk away.

Natalie snagged the end of his shirt just before he stepped out of reach.

"What do you think you're doing telling your brother I'm your girlfriend?" she whispered.

He shrugged, but there was a mischievous smile upon his lips.

"I didn't tell him, he assumed it," he whispered back.

She frowned and lifted her chin. "I noticed you didn't correct him."

Derek put his arm around her waist and pulled her to him. Her breath whooshed out of her in shock.

"Neither did you!" he reminded her, resting the tip of his finger on her bottom lip. The texture of his skin was slightly rough and she wrestled with the inner urge to stick out her tongue for a taste. Or a playful bite.

But she never got the chance. For as quick as he embraced her, he released her, leaving her to catch her breath.

"Because you winked at me!" she accused.

Her knees shook when his eyes tripped over her large breasts with no apology and seemed reluctant to return to her face.

"Oh, is that all I have to do to get you to do what I want?" he teased. "I just need to wink?"

Her cheeks heated at his boldness, not with anger,

but because deep down she liked his attention, even though she knew it was wrong.

Wes called out, "You guys get lost?"

She blew out a ragged breath. "We'll continue this later."

He winked. "I hope so!"

She turned on her heel and strode off, aware of his eyes on her body as he followed close behind.

After holding the kitchen door open for her, Derek pulled out Natalie's chair and she sat.

"Ladies first," he whispered, and the subdued bass in his voice resonated in her ears. He gave her shoulders a little squeeze, and then moved to the other side of the country-style pine table and sat opposite her.

Janet stepped to the table and placed a large bowl of salad and a basket of hot crusty rolls amid the sterling-silver flatware, linen napkins and pretty cobalt-blue plates.

Wes followed with a casserole dish steaming with homemade lasagna. He set it on a trivet right in front of Natalie and the delicious aroma wafted to her and made her appetite soar.

When the couple seated themselves, Derek unfolded his napkin.

"Everything smells and looks delicious," he said, his eyes seeking Natalie's.

She blushed and quickly dropped her gaze. The yearning she felt for him reflected back in the shiny plate in front of her. His simple touch and sensual voice kindled a deep, physical need she'd dare not explore.

Wes picked up some tongs and started to toss the

salad. "Just wait till you taste it. My wife is a wonderful cook."

Janet placed her hands on her hips. "Is that the only reason you married me?" She pouted.

"No way," declared Wes. The tongs clattered against the stainless-steel bowl as he swooped to pull Janet into a kiss.

Watching them embrace, Natalie's face burned with envy. She didn't know how long they'd been married, but it was clear the couple was very much in love. She wished she could experience that kind of relationship. To be swooped off her feet into a passionate kiss at any given moment of the day…

Shame coursed through her and she made a conscious effort to transform her envy into hope. Even though she'd never been blessed with the kind of love that Janet and Wes had, as long as she was alive, there was still a chance.

"Stop it," scolded Janet with a smile on her face. "You're embarrassing me in front of our guests." She put a large slice of lasagna on each plate before retaking her seat.

"Don't mind us," assured Derek. "I'm glad my brother is happy."

"And even happier now that you're here," replied Wes. He bowed his head and folded his hands. "Lord, thank you for moving a mountain and bringing my brother home. May he know how truly loved he is."

"Amen," everyone responded.

Salad and bread were passed around the table. When plates were full, everyone got busy eating.

Natalie groaned inwardly with pleasure. As Wes had promised, the food was delicious. She couldn't recall the last time she had a home-cooked meal. Normally she ate out with clients or friends. There were so many restaurants to try in her Upper East Side neighborhood and New York City in general that she never needed to cook.

Best of all, no cooking meant her kitchen stayed spotless. And Lord knows, she hated to clean.

Derek was the first to break the silence. "Did Pops already eat or is he still putting in overtime?"

Natalie stopped chewing momentarily. Although Derek's tone was casual and unaffected, she knew it was a hard question to ask.

Wes wiped his mouth with a napkin. "He's not here. He moved out ages ago. Before we were even married, right, honey?"

Janet nodded. "We bought the house from him and turned it into a bed-and-breakfast six years ago."

Derek's shoulders slumped and Natalie knew he was disappointed.

"Where's he living now?"

"Above his office," Wes replied.

Confusion leaped into Derek's eyes. "He's living above his office at the school? In the science lab?"

"No, no," Wes said, chuckling. "He quit working there a long time ago—right after you left to play exhibition." He took a sip of water. "He's got his own cleaning business now. People are working for him, instead of the other way around."

Derek whistled in amazement. "Pops has his own business? That was one of his dreams!"

"I know." Wes nodded, his face beaming with pride. "And he's doing really well. He has both commercial and residential contracts."

"That's terrific! Why don't you give him a call and let him know that I'm here."

Janet and Wes looked at each other. To Natalie, it seemed as though a silent message passed between them.

"I don't think that's a good idea, Derek."

Natalie found the anguish in Wes's eyes curious as a storm cloud of tension suddenly moved into the kitchen.

"Why? What's wrong? Don't you want him to know I'm here?"

She could hear the frustration in Derek's voice, even though he tried to hide it.

"He's working his commercial accounts now," Janet interjected a little too hastily. "Businesses are closed down for the night. We probably shouldn't bother him."

Derek looked even more confused. "But I thought you said he had people working for him?"

"He does," Wes reassured him and then laughed. "But you know Pops, he always has to mind the chicken coop and make sure the hens aren't playing when they should be laying eggs!"

Derek half laughed, then shook his head. "How could I forget? He sure wanted to control my life."

Natalie raised her brows at the edge of sarcasm in his voice. Perhaps this was one reason why Derek and his father didn't get along.

Wes speared some lettuce and stuffed it into his

mouth. "We'll get in touch with him tomorrow, okay?" he mumbled between chews.

Derek nodded and picked up his fork.

Natalie noticed he wasn't eating with the same gusto as before, likely due to the fact that the reunion with his father would have to wait another day.

"So what do you do for a living, Natalie?"

"I'm a life coach," she responded, secretly grateful that Janet had changed the subject. "Basically, I help motivate my clients to set goals and do whatever it takes to achieve success in their personal and professional lives."

Janet raised an eyebrow. "Hmm. Maybe you can motivate my husband to put his underwear in the hamper rather than on the floor."

Natalie laughed at Janet's frankness. "I may have a few tips that can help."

Derek looked aghast. "He *still* does that? I remember that I hated going to the bathroom in the middle of the night and stepping on his dirty drawers with my bare feet. I guess some things never change!"

Wes balled up his napkin and threw it at Derek. Everyone burst out laughing. The tension had thankfully disappeared and the men talked sports for the rest of the meal.

Janet stood. "You two must be tired. I'll show you to your room."

"Dinner was wonderful. Can I help you clean up?" Natalie offered.

"Thank you, but that won't be necessary. You're our

guests. Besides, that's Wes's job," she said, tossing him the sponge.

Wes caught it and groaned. "Me and my dishpan hands will see you in the morning."

After they said good-night, Derek grabbed their luggage from the hallway.

Natalie stifled a yawn as they slowly followed Janet single file up the narrow stairs. She couldn't wait to get to her room, strip off her clothes and take a hot, steamy bath.

"The stairs still creak in the same places!" Derek exclaimed, waxing nostalgic.

Natalie smiled and couldn't help but wonder what other memories were hidden in the house.

They went up two sets of stairs and then a smaller set with a low ceiling.

"Are you banishing us to the attic?" she joked.

Finally, Janet stopped and pointed to the sign etched in bronze and gold on the door. "No. Just the bridal suite."

Natalie felt her stomach drop like a runaway elevator. But before she could say anything, Janet turned the knob and ushered the couple into the room.

Natalie blanched at the sight of the elaborately carved antique four-poster bed sitting right in the middle of the small room.

Derek, on the other hand, had a grin as wide as a gambler who'd just won a huge pile of money. How she wanted to punch him!

"But there must be some mistake." The words came out garbled and Natalie coughed a little.

Janet gave her a strange look, likely wondering why Derek's "girlfriend" was making such a stink about sleeping in the same room with her man. Who was, she thought, much hotter in person than he was on television.

"Did Wes take your reservation?" she asked.

"Yes," Natalie said. "I didn't know who it was at the time. I just told the man I spoke to that I was booking accommodations for me and a guest."

"Did you specifically ask for two rooms?"

Natalie racked her brain, but couldn't remember. Probably because she'd been multitasking at the same time she'd made the reservation.

"I'm not sure," she admitted.

"Well, if you had, Wes would have told you that besides this one, there are six other bedrooms and they aren't available. We are completely booked. The local Red Hat Society is here for the weekend."

Natalie was at a loss of what to do or to say. It was too late for her to find a hotel room, although that was exactly what she would do tomorrow. Derek could stay here in the bridal suite and visit his family.

But that left tonight...

Derek put one arm around her waist and hugged her to him. Her insides beamed. Despite the circumstances, it felt wonderful to be held by him again.

"The bridal suite is fine, Janet. We appreciate your hospitality, don't we, sweetheart?"

Natalie nodded, silently reveling in the protective feel of his arm around her waist.

She glanced up into Derek's eyes and saw hot desire.

She could drown in it, in him. Oh, how tempting it was just to take a risk and dive in, to allow him to swallow her whole until she disappeared into the depth of those eyes, his sinew and muscle. Would he taste of briny salt and feel like rough waves moving over her body? Or would their lovemaking be as sweet as teardrops of rain, ending in brilliant sunshine?

Janet took a last look around. "Well, I'll leave you two alone. If there's anything you need, just let me know."

How about a lifeboat? Natalie thought, suddenly gripped with fear. Not at the prospect of spending the night alone with Derek, but at the fact that she'd pushed aside her needs for so long, that she wasn't sure she would have the strength to resist him.

"Good night," they murmured.

When Janet left, Natalie quickly reassessed the situation.

The bridal suite was all bed, all the time. Wide and waiting for two bodies to warm it up.

Derek was all man. Tall and hard, and made for her hands to explore.

Natalie sucked in a breath.

And she was on her own.

Chapter 5

The door clicked shut and the sound, although quiet in reality, echoed in Derek's ears like the roar of his plane's engine. When he was with Natalie, it seemed that everything around him was amplified. He felt more. Both emotionally and physically.

And now it was just the two of them, for one whole night, in the most romantic room in the house. He couldn't think of a more pleasant way to cap off a very long day.

Derek's eyes swept the room.

Candles, roses, a huge four-poster canopy bed and a beautiful woman in his arms.

There were worse things in life.

He'd had the good fortune to be able to have almost any woman he wanted, when he wanted. But none had ever held his interest like Natalie. He was utterly marveled by her, and there was no better time to explore the reasons why than tonight.

He placed his other hand on Natalie's waist and pulled her closer, being careful to keep a small amount of distance between their torsos.

He groaned inwardly. Her tight little body felt as good as it looked, and the painful erection it spurred just then was not the first one of the day. And he was certain it wouldn't be the last.

"Now *this* is awkward," he intoned, stepping a hairbreadth closer to her.

Trying to maintain a respectable distance between their bodies was proving almost impossible. Yet, searching her face, he thought perhaps he'd stepped over a battle line, because right now it looked as if she wanted to slug him.

Natalie's eyes blazed like two torches. "If you're so uncomfortable, then why have you been grinning like a Cheshire cat ever since we got up here?" she accused.

Her breasts swept like a feather against his bare arms as she wriggled out of his grasp. The hair on his arms stood on end and his erection grew even tighter.

A smile broke across his face. She was right. Having her in his arms suited him just fine. Having her sitting astride him, legs cast wide, head thrown back, would suit him even better.

He was a patient man.

Still, because Derek didn't want to risk offending her, he took a half step back, resisting the urge to crush her against his body and never let go. He wanted her to feel his strength, to know the core of his being.

"What can I say?" He shrugged innocently. "When opportunity knocks..."

"You sleep on the couch!" she interjected, poking him in the chest.

"All I see is this big bed. Looks like we're bunking together tonight," he said, a devilish gleam in his eyes.

She crossed her arms. "Guess again!"

"What if you pretend I'm your BFF and we're having a sleepover? You can tell me all your secrets."

His finger roamed the path from her chin to the tip of her earlobe. "I promise I'm a good listener."

She hesitated, then with no response, walked to the mahogany armoire. After opening the doors, she started to rummage through it.

"Do you think it's too late to ask Janet to bring up some extra blankets and pillows?"

"There's plenty on the bed already. How many do we need?"

She looked back and corrected him. "Not 'we.' *You.* The more pillows and blankets you have, the more comfortable you'll be sleeping on the floor."

There was only one place he was going to rest his head, and it wasn't going to be on wood.

He walked over and grabbed her hand. "I promise I won't hog the blankets if you promise you won't snore."

"Not a chance, Derek. I don't sleep with clients."

He thought she would shake his hand away, but she didn't.

That was a good sign.

Instead she closed her eyes and yawned, her feet swaying at the same time.

Instinct took over and Derek put his hand on her shoulder. He steered her to the bed and she sat.

"Are you okay? You almost lost your balance."

"Thanks." She nodded. "I guess I'm just tired."

"We both are," he added.

He sat next to her, suddenly feeling a little guilty, not about his desire for her, but because she seemed exhausted.

"Look, we're two adults. We can handle this situation for one night. Tomorrow we can figure something else out."

"I'm sorry. I should have booked two rooms. I don't know what I was thinking," Natalie said.

"If you had booked two rooms, you probably would have had to give my name," he reminded her. "You wanted to keep this a secret, and it worked. I think my brother was very surprised to see me."

Natalie smiled. "And I'm just glad everything turned out."

"It actually went better than expected." He frowned. "I only wish I could have seen or spoken to my dad tonight."

She rested her hand lightly on his thigh and his skin heated like a lit match all the way to his groin.

"I know that was disappointing, but you'll see him tomorrow."

He sighed and tried to ignore the pleasant feel of her touch. "I guess I should be happy for the extra time.

Maybe by then I'll actually know what to say to him after all these years."

"Any ideas?" she asked, her eyes kind.

He knew his first words should probably be "I'm sorry." But he wasn't sure if he had the courage to say them. He also knew those two words couldn't possibly make up for more than ten years of silence.

He wasn't sorry about the decisions he'd made; he was just sorry about how he'd treated his family to get there. How could he possibly explain it to his father? Pops hadn't listened back then; how could Derek be sure that he would listen now?

"A few," he responded, not sure if he wanted to let her into his thoughts, let alone his heart. His bed? Now that was a no-brainer. From the moment she'd hiked up her skirt and picked up the basketball, he'd wanted her. Plain and simple.

He folded his hand over hers. It felt so small and delicate, as if he held a butterfly in his palm.

Did she have a man in her life? If so, did he treat her well?

"Thank you for pushing me to do this. To see my brother, I mean. I never would have made this trip on my own."

"That's my job," she affirmed in a matter-of-fact voice. "I'm here to support you in this process. And that's it."

She slipped her hand away from his and his skin went cold. It surprised him how much he needed to feel her touch.

"Which side of the bed do you prefer?"

"Any one you don't want," he replied.

She got off the bed and retrieved her suitcase. "I'm going to get ready. Mind if I use the bathroom first?"

He shook his head. "Not at all. Take your time."

She opened a door, inhaling sharply. "This obviously isn't the bathroom."

He pointed to another door. "It's that one. Sorry, I should have pointed that out before."

"No big deal. Where do these go?" she asked, pointing to a narrow set of stairs that wound up out of sight.

"The Turret Room."

She dropped her luggage and craned her head up toward the ceiling. There was a light switch next to the door and she flipped it on, illuminating the stairs.

"Can I see it?" she asked, and the excitement in her voice was unmistakable.

"Sure, though I'm not sure what condition it's in," he warned. But she was out of sight before he'd finished speaking.

He followed her up, taking the stairs two at a time, a little fearful. The last time he'd been in the Turret Room the floor had nearly collapsed under his feet.

Seconds later Derek found her. His throat tightened at the sight of her lush body framed in the moonlight streaming through the windows on all three sides of the turret.

He joined her at the window. She had her nose pressed against the glass, and her knees were perched on the curved window seat. His hands ached to mold the roundness of her upturned bottom with his palms.

He put his hands behind his back and clenched his fists with longing.

"Beautiful, isn't it?"

Only he knew that he wasn't talking about the view outside.

"Mmm-hmm." She nodded without turning her face toward him. "It's like you can see forever."

"Best view in Baker's Falls," he said.

He cranked one of the windows open and the night air wafted in, ruffling the wisps of hair that fell upon her forehead.

"Although the room is small, once you get up here and look out the windows, your whole perspective changes."

She sank down into the seat and slipped her shoes off.

"It's every girl's dream," she said in a faraway voice.

He looked at her curiously. "What do you mean?"

"To live in a castle...in a beautiful room with a turret...waiting for her prince to carry her off on his white horse to be married."

Derek got down on one knee in front of her and placed a hand on his heart.

"This isn't a castle and I don't have a white horse, but I do have the black Jeep you rode in on." He picked up her hand and kissed it. "Will that suit you, milady?"

"Perhaps." She held his gaze, and his heart fluttered crazily. "But then, you'd have to stop being a bad boy. My prince is a one-woman man, not a playboy," she teased.

He sat back on his heels, knowing that while her tone

was playful, the words behind it were not. They lodged like a stone in his stomach.

So that's it, he thought sadly. *She's bought into the hype.*

He couldn't blame her. What she didn't know was that his playboy image was fake, carefully crafted and nurtured by his manager, Tony. The more media coverage about his supposed sexual exploits and party-all-night binges, the more ticket sales went up and the more "attractive" he was to sponsors, and everyone in the league was happy.

Except him.

Deep down, he knew that he wanted one woman whom he could trust enough to give his entire self to. In the past, he'd never reached that point with any woman. His hope that he ever would was fading.

"That'll never happen," he replied, voice dripping with sarcasm.

Natalie's shoulders sagged, as if something deflated within her, and Derek immediately regretted his words.

But it was too late. Although Natalie's eyes were still kind, distrust had moved in, and looked as though it was there for an extended stay.

Once again he'd strengthened the walls of the very image of himself that he wanted to destroy. He suddenly realized that he was so used to squashing his character and denying his needs in the name of money and fame that when he got the chance to be his true self, he screwed things up.

Like right now, he thought.

Natalie stood. "It's a silly dream anyway," she said.

"Thanks for letting me see this room. It's getting late. I'm going to get ready for bed."

She walked away and he was impressed that she was gracious enough not to react in anger to his sudden change in attitude.

"My dad was a prince," he blurted to her back.

She halted and turned around. "What?"

His stomach filled with a strange mix of dread and excitement. Once again, although he wanted to reveal more about himself to Natalie, the prospect of doing so frightened him.

"He bought this house for my mom and not long after..." His voice trailed off. "She left him for another man."

She moved toward him. "Oh, Derek, I'm so sorry. That must have been so hard on you."

It was, but he didn't tell her that. Revealing one skeleton in the closet was enough for now.

"Let me finish the story," he said.

Derek walked to the window and concentrated on the streetlights below, so he wouldn't lose his nerve. He could feel Natalie's presence nearby.

He took a deep breath. "My dad wanted so much more for her, for all of us, than what we had at our crummy apartment. This was his first house and he had a vision for how he wanted it to be, even though he knew it would take a lot of hard work."

He sank onto the window seat. "The morning of the move my mom announced she wasn't coming with us. She claimed the renovations my dad would be doing on the home would make her sick."

"Did she have allergies?" Natalie interrupted.

"Not that we were aware of," Derek replied. "She never even had a cold.

"Anyway, I remember Pops begging her to reconsider, but she wouldn't budge. A couple of weeks later, my dad went back and our neighbors told him she'd moved out just a few days after we arrived in Baker's Falls. They claimed she was with another man. This guy actually used to be a close friend of the family. We never saw her again."

Natalie touched his arm, and the sensation rippled through his body. "That must have been so devastating."

He looked into her eyes and what he saw in their depths was unnerving. It wasn't pity, and he was thankful for that. It was genuine caring.

"Do you know what the worst thing was?"

Natalie shook her head.

"He still loved her after all those years," he said, hating the bitterness in his voice.

"Why did you tell me this, Derek?" she asked.

He took her hand in his. "I just wanted you to know that your dream in itself isn't wrong. You deserve a prince. It's the imperfect people who are expected to make it come true."

"You're right, but you are forgetting one thing," she said.

"What's that?"

"I never said my prince had to be perfect."

Her words hit hard, knocked the breath out of him.

Perfection was something he'd always strived to attain. It's what drove him to succeed and what, ultimately, had destroyed his relationship with his family. The knowledge that he may not have to be perfect to be Natalie's prince was liberating.

Wait a minute, he thought, his mind backtracking. Did he even want to be her prince? He wasn't sure yet, but there was only one way to find out.

"Where do I apply?" he teased.

She tugged on one of his locks. "Who's hiring whom here?" she teased, then sashayed away.

Just before descending the stairs, she paused. "Your dad sounds like a wonderful man. And you know what? I bet he never stopped loving you, either."

Derek leaned against the window, speechless and doubtful.

Natalie didn't know him, but somehow she'd unearthed an emotion he'd forgotten how to feel: hope.

After all these years, it was hard to believe that his dad would still love him. Although he'd dreamed of reconciling with him, he'd never had the courage to do it, until Natalie.

The woman was amazing.

He heard the water go on in the bathroom. A thousand thoughts went through his mind and he stared at the hardwood floor, as if he could see through it to the scene he imagined just below him.

Natalie, her nude body slick with soapy bubbles, relaxed and open. His hands exploring her hot, wet skin. His tongue licking the droplets of steam from her forehead. Their mouths locked together. Water splashing on the floor.

His lips curved into a half smile.

Imperfect people.

Each playing a role in a perfect dream.

Derek knew he was far from being a prince. Yet maybe it was time to work his own kind of royal magic and to show Natalie just how perfect he was for her.

Natalie eased into the antique claw-foot tub and the hot, steamy water enveloped her body, instantly erasing the anxiety of the day and bringing with it thoughts of Derek.

She closed her eyes. The man was as complex as the locks adorning his head. His past was dark and littered with unmet needs. Emotionally, she sensed within him a deep desire for love and attachment. And not necessarily for her, based on his track record.

A lump formed in her throat and, for a moment, she wished things were different. That they'd met under different circumstances. Where there were no boundaries. Professional or otherwise.

A second later she felt foolish. The way she'd talked earlier about finding a prince and living in a castle was so unlike her. She'd given up her girlish dreams a long time ago. Why had she revisited them now? Why should she dream again?

Her eyes fluttered open and she stared at the ceiling.

Because you see something in Derek you want.

She sucked in her bottom lip. More than six feet of hard muscle. That's what she wanted. Nothing more.

Was that so wrong?

She adjusted her body in the water and her nipples poked through the bubbles. The taut peaks of mocha-colored flesh dimpled a little in the air. She dipped her chin to her chest and with soapy hands massaged her breasts freely. With a low moan, she pulled her now-tight nipples upward, as if offering them to the man on the floor above her.

She imagined his body like a ghost floating downward through wood and steel, past wires and pipes, and descending onto her wet flesh with a hunger only he could satisfy.

Her whole body shuddered and she knew she wanted the real thing, the real Derek, not just a fantasy.

Grabbing her mesh sponge, she squirted some of her favorite apricot soap on it and washed her body, hoping that at the same time, she'd wash away her desire for Derek. But the more she rubbed, the more her skin trembled as the material passed over it, leaving her wet, wanting and squeaky clean.

Finally she gave up and stepped out of the tub. If she could get into bed before he did and pretend she was already asleep, she could get through the night without a sexual meltdown.

She toweled off quickly and brushed her teeth. After slipping into her nightgown, she glanced in the mirror and splashed her face with cold water to get rid of the telltale flush in her cheeks.

Upon exiting the bathroom, she tiptoed to the bed, already turned down for the evening, and slipped between the sheets.

She laid ramrod-straight for a few seconds, barely able to keep her eyes open, listening intently. Derek wasn't roaming around upstairs and the house was quiet. Perhaps while she was in the bathroom, he'd gone downstairs to chat with his brother.

While she wanted to wait up for him, the subtle tingling in her body indicated she'd only get herself into trouble if she did.

She reached over and turned off the lamp on the nightstand. Her eyes slid shut and she covered a deep yawn with her hand. As she burrowed her head into the pillows and fell asleep, her last thought was of Derek snuggling right next to her.

A short time later, or it could have been hours, Natalie felt her body being lifted. It hovered for a moment, exposed to time and space and the night air. Her limbs quivered and she wanted to cry out in strange anticipation, but no words came.

Her body was planted and then gently harvested like ripe fruit. She descended, feeling safe, wanting more of the warm cocoon that was her new home.

Roughened fingertips awoke new sensations as they traced her eyebrows, then down the bridge of her nose, only stopping to pause at the vee above her lips, brushing her skin, slightly dry from sleep, below.

Her mouth trembled when those tips took the time to lightly smooth the front of her nightgown free of wrinkles, not wanting to disturb the sleeping beauty.

They hovered over, yet didn't devour or touch her breasts. Instead they seemed to draw strength from the large orbs hidden from sight. Her inner thighs parted involuntarily when roughened tips traveled there, but when they, too, didn't explore, her back arched away from the warmth of the cocoon with subconscious need.

She relaxed again when a palm cupped her flat abdomen and pulled her closer into the cocoon.

"Who are you?" she whispered, her voice round with sleep and pleasure, in her mind or aloud, she didn't know and didn't care. She didn't want whatever she was feeling and experiencing to end.

She stretched her hand behind her and discovered rounded silk. It pulsed and leaped in her palm, and even seemed to grow as she stroked, unaware that the rhythm of her movements was lulling her into a deeper slumber.

She released her hand and burrowed against the iron-stiff hardness resting against her spine. The cocoon growled low, shifted and wrapped her against itself tighter, tasting her skin until just before dawn.

Chapter 6

The next morning, Natalie rolled over in bed and sat up with a startled gasp. She rubbed her eyes in disbelief, but when she opened them, nothing had changed. The other side of the bed appeared untouched. Derek wasn't there.

But how can that be? My dream. Her and Derek. It seemed so real.

Or maybe you just wanted it to be.

Was she delusional?

She slumped back against the pillows in dismay. There was one thing she would admit. She'd missed having a warm body next to her at night. She stretched her arms over her head, still aroused from her dream.

Sunlight filtered through the ruffled curtains and

made triangular shapes on the bed. She was idly counting them when there was a sharp knock on the door.

"Come in," she said.

Derek entered the room, holding a tray. Clad in a pale blue polo shirt and tailored khaki pants, he looked like he could really take charge in a boardroom.

Yet, in Natalie's mind, the man was far too gorgeous to be doing anything but taking charge of her body. In fact, unknown to him, he already had in her dreams. There was an involuntary yet painless tug of need deep in her lower abdomen as he approached the bed.

"Good morning," he said, smiling cheerfully. "I brought you some breakfast."

Before she could react, he set the tray down in front of her on the bed.

She sat up and clutched the covers around her, suddenly feeling self-conscious. Although the cut of her V-shaped nightgown wasn't revealing, just one look at Derek and it felt as though her breasts were bulging out of the fabric.

"What time is it?"

His eyes flitted down, widened slightly and returned to her face.

"A little after nine."

Her cheeks warmed with embarrassment, yet part of her was pleased that he noticed her body.

"You missed the breakfast hour," he continued, his expression friendly. "But lucky for you, I convinced Janet to let me use the kitchen."

She scanned the tray, inhaling lightly. Besides a single rose in a tiny silver vase, there were fresh scrambled eggs, bacon, a blueberry muffin, a bowl of fresh fruit and coffee. Her stomach growled at the feast in front of her. It looked good. A little *too* good.

She met his eyes and her own were skeptical.

"You made all this?" she said, unable to keep the shock and surprise out of her voice.

He reeled back and put a hand on his chest, as if he were offended. "I can do a lot more than bounce basketballs and make coffee."

Natalie pursed her lips. "Oh, really? What else can you do besides make a hot breakfast?"

He plucked the rose out of the vase and sat on the edge of the bed, so close it made her tremble.

"I can make a hot woman—" he dragged the rose lazily along her jawline and then down to the base of her neck "—even hotter."

Her skin flushed. "I'll keep that in mind."

She gently wrested the rose from his fingertips and dropped it back into the vase. "But first, do you mind telling me where you were last night?"

"Why?" he asked, tilting her chin with his fingertips. "Did you miss me?"

Her lips parted. "N-no," she stammered, jerking her chin away. "It's just that Janet said that all the rooms were filled, and I thought we'd agreed to…you know… make the best of things."

He crossed his arms. "Yes, but when I came down from the Turret Room, you'd already fallen fast asleep. You looked so peaceful that I didn't want to disturb you, so I left."

Natalie breathed a sigh of relief. So he had been

there, she thought. Had he merely watched her sleep or had he touched her as he had in her dream?

She narrowed her eyes. "So you didn't get into the bed at all?"

He gave her a strange look and then shook his head. "No, you would have felt it if I had. It can take me a while to get comfortable, especially in a new bed."

She was touched by his concern, but she still couldn't help being disappointed that her dream was just…a dream.

"What's wrong?" he asked.

"I just thought… Oh, never mind. Don't mind me…"

I'm only going crazy.

She took a deep breath. "If you didn't sleep here, then where did you sleep last night?"

Derek covered a yawn with his hand. "A very uncomfortable couch in the parlor downstairs," he replied, the words muffled. "Were people really that short back in those days?"

Natalie laughed. "I'm not sure, but I think that as a whole, they were concerned more about aesthetics rather than comfort."

He stretched and there was a loud crack. "Yeah, my back can attest to that!"

Natalie winced. "Ouch. That sounded like it hurt."

He leaned in close, dreadlocks swaying away from the edge of his shoulders, and whispered lowly, "Not as much as it did to miss the privilege of sharing your bed."

Natalie wanted to say, "There's always tonight," but she also didn't want to encourage him so she kept her thoughts to herself.

Besides, hadn't she planned to find other accommodations for the rest of the weekend? He could stay here in his boyhood home and turn on the mirrors instead of her.

She was glad when, without waiting for her response, he pointed to the breakfast tray. "Dig in, before it gets cold."

As she retrieved the napkin from his hand, the touch between them was electric. He stood and she couldn't help watching his hand quickly brush the wrinkles from the front of his pants.

He bowed. "As much as I don't want to, just like last night, I'll give you some privacy."

Her heart wrestled with her mouth as she watched him walk away. He didn't have far to go. His long legs covered the distance between the bed and the door in two steps.

"Don't leave," she blurted out to his back.

When Derek turned around, a wry smile on his lips, Natalie dropped her head and got busy spreading the napkin across her chest, equally surprised and embarrassed at the urgent tone of her voice.

He knows you want him.

She looked up at his curious stare and immediately classified the thought as ridiculous.

"I mean, why don't we talk about what's on the agenda today while I eat this delicious meal you've prepared for me," she said, speaking in a less intimate tone.

She eyed her plate greedily. She knew what God did on the seventh day. He didn't rest. He created bacon.

She bit into a piece, and almost died on the spot, it tasted so good.

He took a step forward and leaned against the bureau. "I want to go see my father."

She sipped her coffee. "Do you think that's a good idea? It sounded like Wes wanted you to hold off for a while."

Derek nodded. "Yeah, he did, which is exactly why I want to go see him." He pulled out his cell phone and waved it at her. "I got his address and phone number from Wes at breakfast. As soon as you're done, we'll drop by."

She nodded and couldn't help but smile. His excitement was palpable. She could see it in his eyes and she hoped he wouldn't be disappointed. She couldn't imagine why Wes was so leery of Derek seeing their father, but he must have his reasons.

She speared some eggs, chewed and swallowed. "How did the conversation go with Wes? Are you getting more comfortable with him?"

Derek nodded. "Natalie, I'm telling you, it's like I never left." He paused and chuckled. "I haven't seen him since he was a sophomore in high school, but my little brother is the same jokester he always was, just a little bigger around the middle. He claims it's all that good food Janet feeds him, but I think it's something else."

"Like what?"

He stepped to the foot of the bed. "I think he misses playing football. He was a big deal around here when we were in high school. After college, he had the opportunity to play in the pros, but he gave it all up to marry Janet."

"What's wrong with that?" Natalie replied. "They seem happy and very much in love."

He scratched his chin. "I know. But I just have to wonder... Is giving up your dreams for a woman really worth it?"

Natalie looked down as she wiped her mouth and placed the napkin on the tray. To her, the answer was simple.

She raised her eyes to meet his. "I think true love is so rare that when you find it, giving up something for the good of the relationship isn't a sacrifice. It's a gift."

Derek didn't say anything, yet the lost look in his eyes said it all. He didn't believe her. And she didn't understand why that hurt, but it did.

For a second she wished she could retract her words. But they were the truth. Even though she'd never experienced that kind of love, she was always hopeful and she knew she'd give up just about anything to keep hold of it.

She forced a cheerful smile. "I don't think you have anything to worry about, Derek. From what I hear, you can have any woman you want. So I'm sure you can choose one who won't make you give up your basketball career."

Derek reached over, picked up the tray and placed it on the bureau.

"You heard wrong." He sat on the bed and took her hand. "Listen to me," he urged. "All the parties, the late nights, the fake hookups—"

"Wait a minute," she interrupted, slipping her hand from his. "Fake hookups?"

He nodded. "It's all my manager's doing. Tony simply leaks a woman's name to a couple of entertainment bloggers and within hours it's all over the web that I'm dating her." His tongue clicked against his teeth. "I'm always the last one to know."

Her brow knit in confusion. "And what about the parties and the other stuff? Does Tony set those up, too?"

"Some he does. But most times it's just me and the guys from the team getting together and blowing off some steam after the game." He shook his head. "Trouble is, I'm the only one who has a problem getting up in the morning, which is why I'm usually…"

"Late for practice," Natalie finished.

"Right. Tony makes it seem to the media like I'm mayor of my very own Sin City."

"Why does he do it?"

Derek sighed. "In his mind, it's all about marketing. The badder my audience thinks I am, the more ticket sales and endorsement and sponsorship deals I can generate."

Natalie's heart sank. "I still don't understand why Tony hired me."

"He did it to please the owner, to show him that I'm trying to get it together," Derek explained. "There's been rumors of me being traded to another team. If I get traded before my contract is up, Tony loses his stake in the money I bring in. He's finished."

She shook her head. "Wow. It seems like there's more drama in basketball than reality TV."

He laughed and stood. "Anyway, you're off the hook. I'm sure Tony doesn't expect anything good to come out of your coaching sessions. Get dressed and I'll meet you downstairs in a little while."

Natalie pushed the covers off her body and swiveled out of the bed. She wasn't going to let him get away so easily this time.

She caught his hand. "What are you talking about, Derek? I'm not going anywhere until you are reunited with your father. We had an agreement."

"And we still do except… I need to ask you a favor."

"What is it?"

"I don't want to play Tony's game anymore. I need you to help me figure out a way to change my image. I want my fans to know the real me."

"So you don't want to be a bad boy anymore?" she teased.

"Oh, I do," he said. "But only with the right woman. My forever woman."

His forever woman.

The way Derek said those words made her tingle all over. But Natalie knew that to be crowned his forever woman was only a fantasy.

"Derek, I'll help you in any way I can. But," she warned, "you may have to give something up along the way. Do you think you can handle that possibility?"

"With you by my side, I can handle anything."

She smiled, internally glad that he was beginning to have more confidence in her.

Derek picked up the breakfast tray.

His eyes roamed her body, reigniting embers of

arousal, and she felt her knees weaken. "Now, even though you look incredibly sexy in that nightgown, and I've been pretending that it's for my eyes only, I'll let you get dressed."

After he left, she closed her eyes, indulging in the quivers of heat pulsing in her loins.

She'd never wanted a man the way she wanted him.

"I'm not pretending, Derek," she whispered. "If you'll have me, I'm yours."

Derek leaned against the Jeep, waiting for Natalie. He could have stayed inside, but some of the Red Hat ladies were reading and reciting Shakespeare in preparation for the play they were going to see that evening. It was a great excuse to leave so he could watch Natalie walk out to greet him.

Those legs are my paradise, he thought. How he longed to run his hands up and down and between. Last night, he'd dreamed of her legs wrapped around his head as he tasted a sweetness he'd never known.

He hardened instantly at the memory.

It had been so difficult to turn away from her last night. He'd never seen someone look so beautiful just sleeping. He could have lain there all night just looking at her. He wasn't sure he would have the same restraint this evening. Thoughts of Natalie threatened to consume him like a wildfire.

When he got up this morning, his need to see her was so potent that he'd actually made her breakfast in bed.

He chuckled to himself. He'd never gone to the effort for any other woman, so why her? He didn't know, but for the first time in his life, he wasn't afraid to seek the answers.

She approached him then, dressed in a midthigh-length lavender sundress and wedged sandals, both of which set off her lovely legs to perfection. She sauntered slowly, absently, and was searching for something in her purse, unaware that he was watching her from behind his dark sunglasses.

He stood straight, mentally coaxing his erection to behave, although her every footstep toward him was like a lever cranking up his passion for her.

She lifted her head and treated him to a smile that chased away the fears inside him. He'd meant what he said inside earlier. With her by his side, and smiling at him like that, he could face anything.

"Hi. Sorry to keep you waiting. I was looking for my sunglasses, but turns out they were in my purse the entire time."

Natalie slipped on the tortoise-shell frames, then fluffed the top of her short hair, all with the grace and elegance of a debutante.

"No trouble at all," he replied. "I was just enjoying the fresh air."

And looking at you, he added in his mind.

She looked up and shaded her eyes, which was funny since she already had sunglasses on. "Summer's coming early again this year, I guess."

Her dress molded the swell of her breasts, teasing him to stare. He wiped his brow, even though he wasn't sweating.

"I don't mind. I love the heat."

"So do I, which is why I wore this dress. Do you think it's okay for meeting your father?"

Her tone sounded so earnest that he slipped his glasses down the bridge of his nose to appraise her. The diamond heart she wore around her neck glinted in the sunlight. Although her eyes were hidden behind dark sunglasses, he sensed she was seeking his approval, which he was more than willing to give.

"It's perfect. You look beautiful, Natalie."

In that dress, Natalie was like a gift waiting to be unwrapped. He wished more than anything that he could see, touch and taste the treasure beneath.

He hardened again. How was he going to keep his hands off her today?

Her smile widened with pleasure. "Thank you. I hoped you would like it."

After pushing the sunglasses back up on his face, he opened the door. "Let's go."

He helped her into the car. His mind captured the feel of her soft hand and the image of her legs crossing one another as she made herself comfortable. He wanted to remember everything about her and he wanted all the memories of her to be good.

And they would be, just as long as he didn't allow their hearts to be entwined. He knew she wouldn't hurt him. She seemed too sweet for that. But he knew he would eventually hurt her, the way he hurt everyone he loved, and she would never forgive him.

When they had both fastened their seat belts, he started the car and they moved away from the curb.

Now that they were on their way to see his father, his stomach began to churn like a tornado.

Natalie opened the window. "Is your dad's office far from here?"

He drummed his fingers on the steering wheel. "No, just about ten minutes outside of town. Pops always wanted to stay close to his sons, and he thought we would feel the same way."

His mood turned bleak. He thought about how Wes had stayed in Baker's Falls despite having the opportunity to move.

He glanced over at Natalie. "Well, I guess he's got one son who is close by. One out of two isn't bad."

She pushed her sunglasses up on her head and looked at him intently. "What really happened with you two? If you feel comfortable telling me, that is," she added. Her voice was smooth and gentle, coaxing him to reveal more.

Although he wasn't ready to spill his entire life story, deep down he wanted her to know everything about him. He hoped that by helping him to change his bad-boy image, she would discover a man who just wanted to be loved.

His grip tightened on the steering wheel. "My dad always wanted me to go to college. It was his dream. Instead, I decided to enter the NBA draft and he never forgave me."

He shrugged, as if he didn't care, even though he did. "It was that simple."

But it wasn't and he knew it.

He remembered the night of his high school graduation, when he'd told Pops about his decision. It happened right in the kitchen where he'd eaten breakfast this morning. They'd both left the room disappointed and hurt. And they'd never spoken again.

The old anger suddenly gelled inside.

"Do you know how many fathers would die to have their sons playing in the NBA? It's every dad's dream! It was my dream! I never understood why he was unhappy about my decision."

After all these years, Derek couldn't believe how much it still hurt inside to think, or even to talk about what happened. He wondered if he'd ever get over his anger and resentment.

Natalie touched his arm and he immediately felt calmer and more peaceful. He was beginning to like the effect she had on him.

"Maybe he knew that someday the dream would end," she offered. "Maybe he wanted you to be prepared for that day, so you would know what to do in the next phase of your life."

He blew out a breath. "I'll never quit playing basketball," he insisted.

But that was a lie. As he got older, the likelihood that he would suffer serious injury increased. The game of professional basketball, like any other professional sport, was just hard on the body. Period.

How many more years did he have before his reflexes started to be less than keen and his bones ached for longer than a day? It was time he accepted that someday his jersey would be retired. What would he do then? He truly didn't know.

"Pops said I would regret my decision someday."

"Well, do you?"

He thought a minute. He didn't regret the great teammates he'd had, some of whom had become great friends, or the cities he'd traveled to, or the money he'd made over the years.

The women he'd met? He'd never expected to fall in love with any of them. Until Natalie.

His heart raced. Was that what he was experiencing now? Was he falling in love with her?

His suspension was only for three games and then he was back on the court. He'd hardly had the chance to get to know her. Yet he knew it was best to tamp down the feelings, if that's what they were, rising within him.

There were too many things that would get in the way of loving her. His travel and practice schedule, late-night games, the paparazzi and the press. But he knew those were only excuses for the truth: he couldn't bear disappointing someone else he loved. Deep down he knew that's why he never got serious about any woman, why he consistently brushed them aside in favor of his first love. In his heart, he knew he couldn't have both: a serious relationship and a career in basketball.

Falling in love would mean he'd have to give something up and he wasn't sure he was ready.

Would Natalie ask him to give up his career in the NBA? He remembered that she thought true love brought with it the gift of sacrifice. Just thinking about not playing basketball made his heart drop in his chest. After that, he just felt empty.

True love would have to wait.

"The only regret I have is hurting my dad," he responded thickly as he pulled into the nondescript parking lot of Lansing Commercial Cleaning Services. The one-level brick building in front of them was nicely landscaped. He cut the engine and stared straight ahead.

"Derek?" Natalie asked. "Are you all right?"

He slowly put his sunglasses on the dashboard, then leaned back against the seat.

"I don't know what to say to him."

Derek looked at the building and gripped the steering wheel, trying but failing to keep the panic out of his voice. "Tell me, Natalie. What do I say?"

She reached over and turned his face toward hers with her palm. His breath rushed out of him with surprise. Her movements were bold, yet her touch was soft and caring.

"Just say what's in your heart," she whispered.

When she released his face, his emotions were churning and he felt as if she'd opened his eyes to what had been there all along. He just couldn't see it.

Without thinking, he cupped his hand around her neck and the world seemed to disappear as he closed his eyes and guided her lips to his. They tasted of ripe peaches, a sun-radiant burst of glorious wonder.

His movements were tentative at first. He wanted to focus on her rather than on the intense need she drove within him.

The need to devour.

She leaned into him, kissing back unrestrainedly, and he wanted to shout with joy. The tip of his tongue dipped into her mouth and she groaned. Opened deeper.

So he slid inside and discovered a velvety warm place he wanted to explore forever.

Abruptly he ended the kiss and leaned back in his seat.

"I just wanted to show you what was in *my heart,*" he said in a low voice.

Natalie nodded, her eyes dancing with mutual desire. He gazed at her lips, full and ripe. His kiss was only a glimpse of what he was starting to feel for her, a sneak preview of the sensual experiences he wanted to have with this woman.

But she deserved more than just one night with him. She deserved a lifetime of love. And he knew he wasn't ready to give that to her yet. Maybe he never could.

Without another word, he got out of the car.

He opened the passenger door, the taste of her mouth still on his lips. He could fall in love with that taste. With her.

"Let's go before I kiss you like that again."

She smiled and he took her by the hand, and they walked into the building together.

The receptionist greeted them. "How may I help you?"

She took no special notice of Derek and for once, he was glad he wasn't recognized.

Reluctantly he let go of Natalie's hand. "I'm here to see James Lansing."

She looked at the couple and then turned to her computer screen. "Do you have an appointment?"

Just then, a door down the hall opened. His heart lifted when he spotted his father walking toward him, limping slightly. Derek racked his brain for a moment, trying to remember if Pops had walked like that when he and his brother were younger.

The secretary swiveled in her chair.

"Oh, Mr. Lansing, there you are," she said cheerfully. "You have a visitor." She put a fist to her mouth. "Oh, but I didn't ask his name, silly me." She turned back to Derek. "What is your name, sir?"

His father stood a few feet away, but the emotional chasm was wider, with years of hurt and pain between them.

At first neither man said a word and it seemed as though the room had narrowed until there was no sense of time at all. Derek was certain that if Natalie wasn't standing by his side, he would have turned tail and run.

His father was the first to speak.

"I already know his name," he said in the same stern tone he'd used when Derek was a child. "And you can tell him I'm busy. My schedule is booked today and for the rest of my life."

Derek sucked in his stomach, helpless against a mix of hatred and fear bubbling inside as he watched his dad limp back down the hall to his office.

Derek slammed open the front door so hard he almost broke the glass, but he didn't care. He just wanted to get away. From his dad, from the look of confusion, but mostly from the look of pity on the secretary's face, on Natalie's face, from everyone and everything.

I should have never come back here.

Tears stung his eyes as he ran.

"Derek, wait!" Natalie shouted, desperation in her voice.

He looked back and she was running after him, as best as she could in those heels of hers.

He stopped, concerned that she would fall and break an ankle. He did not want her to get hurt; he didn't need any more pain on his conscious. He had enough to last three lifetimes.

While she was still a long way off, he bent at the waist and wiped at his eyes, hoping Natalie would think it was sweat. What would she think seeing the bad boy of basketball crying?

When she caught up to him, he straightened and turned, his face burning with anger and shame.

"Derek, I'm—" Natalie's voice broke.

Her eyes, pleading and sorrowful, nearly tore him to pieces inside. Somehow he knew she *understood.* But he didn't know why and at this point, he didn't care. All he could feel was his own pain. "Sorry?" He smirked, knowing full well he sounded bitter and mean. "Remember when you said that family always forgives?"

She nodded, her eyes welling with tears.

"Well, you were wrong," he stormed, his words as hard and impenetrable as the stone in his heart.

He reached into his pocket and tossed her his car keys. "Take the Jeep back to Belle Amour and wait for me there," he commanded, ignoring the hurt look on her face.

And before she could say anything, he took off running and he wasn't sure if he would ever go back.

Chapter 7

Natalie arrived back at the bed-and-breakfast a few minutes later, still in shock. Her heart ached for him, knowing how disappointed he was feeling right now. Plus, he was angry with her and at some level she felt she was to blame for the negative outcome of their reunion.

She couldn't blame Derek for being angry at her. On the drive back, she realized she'd made an error in judgment. Although her intentions were good, she'd probably set high expectations in his mind, without knowing the complete history of Derek's estrangement with his family. No wonder she wasn't practicing psychology anymore.

With her head down, she walked toward the house, idly kicking pebbles out of her way along the stone path.

"What's wrong, pretty lady?" Wes called out.

She looked up, startled, and hurried onto the porch. "Oh, I didn't see you there."

He laid the paper across his broad belly. "I noticed," he replied. "Where's Derek?"

When she didn't respond, he tossed the paper on the floor.

"Oh, no. He went to go see Pops, didn't he?"

To Natalie's ears, Wes's voice sound strained and tinny, almost fearful.

She sat on the porch swing and kicked out her feet. It began to sway back and forth.

"Yes, and it didn't go well. Your dad basically slammed the door in his face," she said in an accusatory tone.

If she sounded upset, it was because she was. She remembered the contrite look on Derek's face when he'd seen his father for the first time in years. Couldn't the man at least have *talked* to Derek?

Wes leaned on his knees with his elbows, covered his face and said nothing for a few seconds. When he took his hands away from his face, he looked ill.

"How did Pops look? Did he seem sick?"

Natalie thought that was a strange question. "I don't know. I guess he looked fine. I only saw him for a few minutes. Why do you ask?"

"No reason." Wes looked away and that's when Natalie knew he was hiding something.

"What's going on, Wes?" she asked.

"Nothing I can't handle," he assured her. "Where's Derek now?"

She frowned. "I don't know. He told me to drive back here and wait for him.

"Derek was so hurt," she continued, her eyes filling with tears. "I'm worried about him, Wes."

Wes stood and grasped the porch railing. He looked down the street. "Maybe I should go after him." His voice sounded distracted, as if he was talking to himself rather than Natalie.

"Would you?" she asked, her tone hopeful.

Wes turned and leaned against the railing, seeming to weigh his options. She knew he'd changed his mind when he sat on the wicker chair and picked up the paper again.

"He won't get far on foot," he declared. "Baker's Falls is a small town. I'm sure he'll come back when he's ready."

She started to protest, but Wes interrupted her.

"Sometimes a man needs to be alone with his feelings before he can share them with someone else."

She smiled, but only because his words of wisdom made sense.

"Hmm. Does that trait run in the family?"

"Nah," he replied gruffly. "I wear my heart on my sleeve. Ask Janet."

She laughed, even though in the back of her mind she knew both he and Janet were keeping some kind of secret about "Pops."

Right then and there, she vowed to find out what it was. If she could prevent Derek from getting hurt any more, that's exactly what she would do.

She folded her legs up under her body, getting as comfortable as she could on the hard wooden bench.

"Do you mind if I wait for Derek out here with you?"

He shook his head. "Not at all."

She tilted her head toward the floor. "Anything going on in the news besides war, politics and the economy?"

"Oops, how'd you get there?" he joked, stooping to pick up a section of the newspaper that lay scattered on the blue-painted wood.

He gathered it up and folded it neatly. "Nah…just the sports section. I don't play football anymore, but I like to keep up with what the guys out there on the field are doing."

She nodded. "I can understand that."

"It was also the way I kept up with Derek." His voice softened. "I missed my brother, Natalie. Thank you for bringing him home."

"You're welcome," she replied. "I'm just sorry the reunion with your father didn't go so well."

Wes looked away and snapped open the newspaper. "Pops will come around," he boasted loudly. "I'm sure he was just shocked to see him."

She raised her eyebrows at his keen interest in the paper. She knew he couldn't possibly be reading because the paper was upside down.

Crossing her arms, she wondered why whenever she talked about Pops, Wes wouldn't make eye contact. Plus his reaction was a little too confident, as if he could tell the future. What was he hiding?

A few minutes later Wes lowered the paper again.

"Say, you missed breakfast and lunch. Do you want me to make you a sandwich?"

She shook her head. "No, thank you. I'm really not hungry. I think I'll go up to the room and lie down."

Wes nodded. "Okay. Listen, if you see Derek before I do, tell him BFA is playing tonight against Glen Castle. Maybe he can make an appearance?"

"BFA? Bachelor of Fine Arts?"

Wes's laughter could have woken the dead.

"No. I forgot you're not a local. BFA stands for Baker's Falls Academy, our old alma mater. Glen Castle High School was, and still is, one of our biggest rivals."

"I'll tell him," she replied. "See you later."

She walked in, letting the porch door slam behind her. She trudged up the stairs, annoyed with Wes for keeping secrets from Derek. Plus, how could he be thinking about a silly high school rivalry at a time like this?

His brother had gone to his father as a prodigal son, and had been totally rejected. And all Wes could think about was sports?

She threw her purse on the bed and slipped off her shoes before heading up to the Turret Room.

"I can see where his heart is," she muttered aloud.

But when she looked out the window and saw Wes hop into his truck and speed down the street, she wanted to take back her words.

Wes clearly loved his older brother.

The question was: Did she?

She brought her fingers to her mouth and shivered. *That kiss!*

Now that time wasn't a dream, she mused. But she wished his lips would claim hers forever.

The man was so fine. She yearned to feel the muscles that lay under every inch of his skin.

But there was the trouble of his image—the one he claimed he wanted her to change. It wasn't that she had a problem with bad boys. It's just that most of them didn't stick around long enough to have any type of meaningful relationship.

Is that what she wanted? she asked herself. A relationship with Derek?

She placed her forehead against the glass, warmed by the midday sun.

"I don't know," she said aloud.

"Don't know what?"

She whirled around, surprised. "Derek!"

He lifted his hands. "The one and only!"

She wanted to rush over to him with a hug, but stopped herself. And not because he was dripping with sweat.

She didn't want to pressure him into talking about what went down with his dad. She wanted to give him time to sort out his feelings. As far as she was concerned, they had all the time in the world.

"Are you okay?"

"Yeah." He nodded, but something in his manner told her otherwise. He was too calm. It was almost as if he was walking a tightwire, trying not to fall off.

"Where were you?" she asked, trying to keep her voice casual, even though she'd been worried about him.

He shuffled his feet. "I decided to go for a run

through town, but I forgot these clothes aren't exactly marathon material."

He pulled at the collar of his shirt. "It's boiling up here. Mind if I get rid of this?"

She hadn't noticed the temperature of the room until he peeled his wet polo away from his body and tossed it on the floor without waiting for her answer.

Her eyes grazed the tight muscles of his broad, hairless chest, down to the abdomen cut with a six-pack of perfection, and below, where her imagination, and her hands, were bound to go wild.

It's definitely hot up in here now.

"Will you show me Baker's Falls? I'd love to see the town."

He shrugged and seemed distracted. "Sure, if we have time."

"What are you talking about?"

He looked uncomfortable. "I planned on flying us out tonight." His voice dipped low. "There's no reason for me to stay in Baker's Falls."

Her heart lurched and felt the pain he tried to mask. "What about Wes? He just went out looking for you."

"He'll come back in time for dinner." He stepped toward her. "Besides, we talked at breakfast. He wants to come and visit me in New York. At least *he* wants to see me, unlike my father," he added bitterly.

"Give him time, Derek."

He gave her an incredulous look. "Why should I? He hates me."

"Derek, I'm sure he doesn't hate you," she said, trying to reassure him.

He backed up and leaned against the wall. "Oh, no? Well you must not have seen the look in his eyes. Like I told you before we even got here, he doesn't want anything to do with me!"

She thought about Wes's reaction earlier. "Maybe he has something going on in his life right now. Something he's trying to deal with."

Derek jammed his hands into his front pockets. "What could be so important that he can't talk to me? His own flesh-and-blood son whom he hasn't seen in years?"

She shook her head. "I don't know, Derek, but I think that instead of throwing in the towel, you should wait it out for a while. Maybe he just needs some time to process things."

He shouldered himself from the wall and strode over to her, his eyes fiery with hurt. "Look, what's done is done. Why can't you accept that?"

She crossed her arms and stood her ground. "Because I won't and neither should you."

He closed his eyes and lifted his chin toward the ceiling.

"People can change, Derek," she said softly, admiring the strength of his jawline. On impulse, she reached out her hand and traced it gently. "You did," she reminded him.

He opened his eyes and she took his hand. "Maybe your dad has, too. You just have to give him time to show it."

He didn't respond. Instead his eyes examined her face, seeming to want to memorize her every feature.

"You care about my life, right?"

Her stomach clenched at the serious tone of his voice. She squeezed his hand. "Of course, Derek. I care about the lives of all my clients."

He stepped closer, so that their bodies were mere inches away from each other. The scent of his sweat was surprisingly arousing, and she felt her nipples pucker under her dress.

"Is that all I am to you?" he asked, caressing her cheek as though it was fine silk. "A client?"

"No," she responded, resting her cheek in his palm. He stroked it gently, and his touch caused her to sigh inwardly. "I care about you as a person."

He closed the gap between them. When she felt the hard length of his desire against her abdomen, her knees went weak.

He cupped her face. "Anything else?"

"Yes," she said, slipping her hands around his waist. On impulse, she moistened her lips and kissed the tight muscle of his left breast. It flexed under her mouth and tasted of salt.

"I care about you," she whispered, moving her lips slowly up to the base of his neck. "As a man."

At that moment he pulled her even closer and uttered a loud groan. The sound of the pleasure she was giving him tickled her lips, and she felt the vibrations all the way through her body.

Suddenly he pushed her away, breathing hard. "That's what I thought."

Her eyes stole a look at his torso where the outline

of his physical need for her was clearly evident beneath his khakis.

"Did I do something wrong?" she asked.

He ran a hand over his head and shook it side to side. "No, no, you did everything right."

His eyes trailed over her body, and the intense heat from his gaze made all of her inner places moisten.

"God help me." His breath was ragged. "I can't hurt you, too."

She started toward him. "You'd never hurt me," she said, reaching out her hands. She needed to be held by his strong arms. But more importantly, she needed to hold him.

"Derek, I'm confused. Tell me what's going on."

He backed away, splintering her heart.

"I'm sorry, my mind is made up. Pack up because we're leaving. I want to be back in New York by this evening. I'm going to hit the shower."

And before she could say anything, he picked up his shirt, tossed it over his shoulder and went down the stairs.

She sank onto the window seat, feeling aroused and rejected.

Now what? she thought. She couldn't let him quit. She had to convince him to stay.

Because he's your client? her mind asked.

"No, because I love him," she whispered.

Thirty minutes later Derek stepped out of the shower and wrapped a towel around his waist. Despite the lukewarm water, his arousal had only half subsided. But his

desire for Natalie was as strong as ever. He was falling for her. Hard.

The woman who as a child dreamed of being a princess deserved more than he could ever give her. The only choice he had was to leave. This way, neither of them would be hurt.

He squirted a few drops of coconut oil in his hand and massaged it into his locks, wishing he could spread it all over Natalie's body. She was such a temptress.

After a quick shave, Derek patted on some aftershave and brushed his teeth. Closing his eyes, he remembered the way she'd responded to his kiss. The feel of her soft lips on the bare skin of his chest. The woman was too hot to handle only one time. He knew if he made love to her, once would never, ever, be enough.

He dropped the towel down the laundry chute, then looked around for his change of clothes and cursed. He'd been in such a hurry he'd forgotten to take them out of his suitcase. Hopefully, Natalie was either still upstairs or not in the room.

He put his ear to the door and heard nothing. The coast was clear.

He stepped out of the bathroom, nude and trying not to think of her. Though the shades were drawn and the bedroom was half darkened, he immediately spotted her lying on the bed and she was fast asleep.

Just like last night, he thought.

He sucked in a breath, knowing he had two choices. Reason told him to quietly get his clothes, get dressed and get out of there. But his body told him otherwise. And what he felt in his heart for Natalie sealed the deal.

He was falling in love with her.

He wanted her.

He would have her.

Derek gathered his locks into a ponytail before moving forward. He stepped as lightly as he could so the floorboards wouldn't squeak and awaken her.

He stood by the bed, watching her, fulfilling a fantasy.

She was lying half on her side, half on her back. Her sundress was hitched up almost to the top of her thighs, her chest moving up and down in rhythm with her breathing.

But it was her mouth that did him in. Slack and slightly open. Ready. Tempting him even in her slumber.

He lay next to her, as lightly as possible, even though his six-foot-six frame wanted to pounce on her like a tiger.

He trailed his finger down her slender nose.

She opened her eyes, questioning. Desiring.

And at that moment, he was lost.

"Forgive me," he begged, and placed his mouth over hers, laying claim. Ripe and juicy, and all for him. He palmed her face, stroked her cheeks and tasted greedily.

Her tongue joined with his, took charge. She licked the outside corners of his mouth so slowly he could feel the ridges of her taste buds.

His body convulsed erotically with the new sensation. Such a simple display of affection, but no woman had ever done that before. He wondered what other surprises she had in store for him.

She bit his bottom lip and they both moaned.

He rolled on top of her and she encircled her arms around his waist and pulled him closer. Kissing him deeply, slowly.

Suddenly, Natalie broke away.

"It's not fair," she moaned, pouting.

He leaned up on one elbow and smiled. Her heart-shaped mouth was formed in the most perfect little O he'd ever seen.

"What's not fair, sweetheart?" he asked, edging the shape of her lips with his thumb.

She ran her fingernails lightly over his bare chest, traced a tiny circle around his nipple. His chest muscles tightened in response and he dropped his head back, breathing hard.

"You're the only one who's naked."

He brought her head slowly down to his and sucked on her petulant lips. "So what do you want me to do about it?" he murmured.

"Take off my dress," she commanded.

He took his lips from hers. "With pleasure."

The mattress bowed beneath him as he got to his knees. When he bent his head and kissed her legs, they were as soft and as smooth as he'd dreamed. His lips glided over and over her upper thighs, exploring.

With his hands, he pulled her legs apart.

With his nose, he pushed the lavender fabric of her dress up and out of the way. He sucked in a breath.

Natalie was full of surprises, for she wore no underwear.

Had she been like that all day? When he'd kissed

her in the car? Not knowing the answer excited him even more.

He buried his face in her. She cried out, guiding his mouth from her tight spirals to her moist flesh. She was well prepared. So wet already that he almost lost control. It was too soon for that and he was tempted to pull away. But he didn't.

Instead he burrowed deeper. He was where he wanted to be at that moment, where she needed him to taste.

So he tasted. And sucked. And drank the juice of her desire for him. Holding on to her by the waist as she writhed and twisted. And he throbbed and grew.

She bolstered herself up on her elbows and sank back into the pillow again as he treated her to another wave of pleasure.

"My dress, remember?" she gasped.

He broke away and lifted the dress up and off her body and onto the floor, where it should have been all along.

He unhooked the front clasp of her bra, got his first look at her breasts, and his mouth went dry. Caramel-colored delight. Her dark nipples tipped up, as if ready to pass his inspection. He kissed each one politely, just a little peck that seemed to drive Natalie wild.

She wriggled her hips sensuously beneath him, clamped her hands on his buttocks and squeezed as if she never wanted to let go.

When she grasped a breast in each hand, ran her thumbs around in circles, teasing him to devour the hardened tips, he held back. Even though it was difficult, he wasn't taking orders from her this time.

"Lie on your back," she commanded.

He smiled.

Except that one, he thought, and obliged her.

She scrambled up and sat back on her heels, her breasts round and firm and beautiful.

It was her turn to inspect him, and by her gasp of wonder, he knew he'd passed with flying colors.

He'd never been harder for or wanted any woman as much as he wanted Natalie.

He reached for her and his eyes widened as she lifted one thigh over his waist to sit astride him.

His flesh throbbed painfully as it lay against the crease of her hot buttocks, hard weight cushioned by soft skin.

Suddenly she got up, crouched flat on her heels and braced her hands on his chest. She spread her legs wide and lowered herself slightly. She didn't have to go far when her moist flesh made contact with his.

He made a guttural sound. "Natalie," he groaned, reaching to help her.

She stopped his hand before it even made it halfway down his body.

"Shh." She cooed and put her finger on his lips. "Let me do this, please?"

Quietly. Slowly. And oh, so completely, she sheathed him. Encased him in the moist, warm darkness of her inner flesh. The sweetness he'd tasted within her was now completely his.

He could barely breathe. Every muscle in his body tensed with indescribable pleasure, and his mouth dropped open. He wanted to yell, but there was no sound he could make that could possibly match what he was feeling right now.

And then…she rode him.

Chapter 8

There's nothing like knowing you've completely satiated your man, Natalie thought, gazing down at Derek.

She lay upon him, still holding the towering core of his body within her own, while his muscular legs splayed out beneath her and continued to quake in the aftermath of their passion.

She rocked to and fro gently, selfishly. Milking the moment, not wanting to release him or to stop.

"Still want to jump in a plane and leave?" she whispered into his ear.

"God, no," he replied, reaching for her breasts. His breathing was agitated, but his tone was deep with satisfaction. "I want more."

Their bodies still moved, slower and more deliberate now, but everything had changed. Neither of them knew whether it was for better or for worse. And for the moment, neither of them cared.

A sharp knock on the door abruptly ended their embrace.

"Derek," shouted Wes. "Are you in there?"

"Yeah," Derek responded in a thick voice.

"Open up," Wes commanded.

They looked at each other and Natalie reluctantly slid from Derek's body, then scrambled for the covers. Derek grabbed a pair of white boxers from his suitcase and stepped into them.

He peeked his head out the door. "What's going on?"

Since the door was only cracked open, all she saw was Wes's beefy arms waving frantically.

"I spent two hours looking for you all over town, man. Natalie told me you'd gone to see Pops and were upset. Why didn't you call me or tell me you were back home?"

Derek cracked the door open a little wider. "Does this explain things?"

Natalie squealed and sat up in bed, covering her breasts with the sheets just before Wes leaned to the side and spotted her.

He tipped his baseball hat in her direction. Her face burned and she nodded back, wanting to crawl under the covers and hide.

"Aw, man. I'm sorry to interrupt," he said, sounding thoroughly embarrassed. "I was just worried, that's all."

He elbowed Derek and smiled. "I'm glad you're okay, bro."

Wes tipped his baseball cap at Natalie. "Take care of him, okay?"

Derek looked back at her. "She already has, trust me."

His wicked smile set her imagination on fire and she wanted to jump out of bed and go to him, no matter who was watching.

"Say goodbye, Wes," he said.

"Hope to see you guys at the game!" Wes shouted just before Derek closed the door in his face.

Derek leaned against the wood and Natalie let the covers fall away.

"Now where were we?" he asked, eyeing her hungrily.

She swung her legs over the bed and got up. Her knees wobbled as she walked toward him.

She clasped her arms around his waist. "Going to the game," she said, pecking him on the lips. "Your alma mater is playing tonight. Wes told me about it earlier, but I forgot to tell you."

"I wonder why," he teased, cupping her bottom and pulling her closer.

She laughed. "I think we should go. It would be good for you to make an appearance."

His smile disappeared. "I don't know, Natalie. What if my dad is there? I can't take another run-in with him. At least not right now."

She took a step back. "But I thought your brother said he didn't work at the school anymore."

"He doesn't," he replied. "But you don't understand.

Pops is a huge basketball fan. When I played high school ball, he never missed a game."

"What about your professional career?"

His frown deepened. "As far as I know, he's never seen me play in the NBA."

"I'm sorry, Derek."

He placed a finger on her lips. "It doesn't matter anymore. Let's not ruin an amazing afternoon by talking about him, okay?"

She hoped what she was about to say wouldn't upset him.

"But going back to your old school may help you to accept some of the things that happened between you and your dad."

He looked unconvinced. "I don't see how."

"Let's go and I'll show you." She squeezed his hand. "Besides, it'll be fun," she added. "I like imagining what you were like when you were younger."

Derek crossed his arms. "I'll go on one condition. If my dad shows up, we're out of there. Agreed?"

She wasn't going to go back to New York until the reunion was complete. She didn't know what was wrong with his father this morning, but tonight could be another chance for Derek and his dad to talk things over.

Baby steps, she thought, nodding in agreement.

"How about some pregame excitement?" He winked. "Let's go have some fun with bubbles."

He flashed a devious smile and she shrieked as he swooped her up and nestled her in his arms like a bride, kissing her full on the mouth. It had been an unforgettable afternoon that she wished could last forever.

* * *

The parking lot was jam-packed when Derek and Natalie pulled up to Baker's Falls Academy. When they found a space, they got out of the car and both stared at the black iron gate and stone wall that surrounded the cluster of historic buildings. The school looked like something out of the movies: formidable, foreboding and very, very rich.

Natalie could only imagine what going to a private school must have been like for Derek, who'd grown up in one of the poorest areas of New York City. She found it ironic that years later, he was probably wealthier than most of his classmates.

Deep in her heart, she wished he were happier, too.

"This place is like a whole other world," she commented.

"Yeah. When my dad first drove us here," Derek recalled, "I felt like I was Will Smith in *The Fresh Prince of Bel-Air,* but without the goofy hat. Know what I mean?"

His voice sounded light and uneasy at the same time. He took her hand in his and they started to walk toward the gymnasium.

She chuckled. "I used to love that show. Were you the only African-American?"

He shook his head. "There were a few of us already here. My brother and I both went here on athletic scholarships, but it didn't cover everything. My dad still had to work two jobs in order for us to go to school here."

"That must have been hard on him."

"Yeah, but I didn't realize it. Back then, I was just ashamed of him."

He stopped walking and seemed to debate something in his head. "Can you imagine how embarrassing it would be knowing that your dad is the school janitor?"

His words stung the air and pierced her heart, even though they had nothing to do with her.

She put her hands on her hips. "Why? Because he cared about you?"

He looked at her as though she had two heads. "I lived with the fear that at any moment, while I was walking to class with my friends, we would come around a corner and see my dad with a mop and a bucket in his hand," he said, ashamed that the old tone of disgust had slipped back into his voice.

"Did that ever happen?"

"Of course. He'd always hang around the basketball courts, too."

"Maybe that was the only place he felt close to you," she said quietly.

He ran his hand down his face, as realization set in. "I sound so selfish, don't I?"

She said nothing, knowing that he already knew the answer.

"I know this doesn't excuse my attitude, but that's how I felt as a kid," he explained.

"But you're not a kid anymore. How do you feel about your dad now?"

Derek thought for a moment, then smiled. "Proud."

He kissed her lightly and they began to walk again.

At the entrance, Derek hesitated. "This place is so full of memories, both good and bad."

She took his hand. It trembled a bit in her palm. "So let's go make some new ones together, okay?"

He nodded and smiled in agreement. And right now, that was enough for her.

As soon as they opened the door Natalie heard someone shout, "Hey, there's Derek Lansing!" and the crowd engulfed the couple as they tried to make their way down the hallway to the gym.

Natalie saw heads turn and crane for a look at the handsome NBA pro. Cell phones were out and she imagined some of the kids were texting about the scene in one hundred and twenty characters or less.

She almost laughed aloud at the thought of Derek's manager, Tony, hearing about the couple from a teenage tweeter, rather than through his own dishonest means. What Tony didn't know or realize was that Natalie and Derek's relationship wasn't manufactured for a media buy.

It was real.

At least in her mind it was. At the moment she had no way of knowing if Derek felt the same way.

Suddenly, Wes appeared from out of nowhere and ushered the couple into the boys' locker room.

One of the players whistled at Natalie.

"Should I close my eyes?" she asked Derek.

"Not necessary," he said. "Looks like most of the team is out on the floor."

He turned to his brother. "What's going on, Wes? I

haven't seen this place so excited since we won the state championships way back when."

Wes shrugged. "I guess word got around you were stopping at the game."

"Let me guess. The messenger was you," Derek accused good-naturedly.

"It didn't help that you were jogging all around town earlier," Wes scoffed, punching Derek in the arm. "Like a giant billboard."

Derek looked around. "Is Pops here?"

Wes shook his head, then changed the subject.

"What's the matter, man? It's not like all this attention is new to you."

Natalie saw a hurt look cross Wes's face, and she knew it wasn't from jealousy. She had a feeling he'd prepared this little homecoming celebration for his big brother, but Derek was so wrapped up in avoiding their father, he hadn't even noticed.

The two brothers had only been reunited yesterday. She hoped this minor misunderstanding wouldn't come between them.

She breathed a sigh of relief when Derek clapped Wes on the shoulder. "It's okay. I just wasn't expecting it."

The two men smiled and shadow-boxed each other for a few seconds. Another family crisis was averted and all was forgiven.

Wes wiped his brow and checked his watch. "Come on, it's almost time for tip-off."

He led them to the gym where a couple of thousand people were gathered. The excitement in the air was palpable. It was so loud in there that Natalie was tempted to put her hands over her ears.

A few seconds later she spotted Janet waving at her frantically. After she told Derek where she was headed, she made her way to the stands where Janet was saving her a seat.

Natalie sat and blew out a breath. "Thanks. I didn't think I'd make it up here alive. Is it always this crazy in here?"

"Only when Derek Lansing is in town," Janet responded with a laugh. "Any other Friday night the decibels are fairly manageable."

Natalie laughed and looked around. They were surrounded by teenagers who were full of the energy and sense of life that comes with not having any real responsibility.

"It feels strange being in a high school."

"Where did you grow up?"

"Manhattan," Natalie replied. "When I was younger, I was an ice-skater, so I was mostly homeschooled during my school years, or I had tutors on the road."

Janet's face lit up. "I *thought* I recognized you."

"You do?"

"Yes. I used to take figure skating lessons when I was a child. You were one of my favorite pros."

"Thanks!" Natalie was astonished and a little embarrassed. She didn't run into too many people who knew her from the old days. And that was fine by her.

"I hope you don't mind me asking, but I've always wanted to know one thing. Why were you called the 'Ice Queen'?"

She wanted to say that she'd earned the moniker because, as a professional skater, she'd commanded the ice.

But that would have been a lie. During her formative years on the ice, she'd made her share of mistakes. She'd had plenty of triple lutzes, one of the most difficult skating moves, turn into triple klutzes and she'd ended up on her butt.

No, the real reason was that she was so focused on skating, on being the best, that she wouldn't let anyone get close to her. Not her coach, her teammates or the audience.

Her heart clenched in her chest. Not even her parents, she remembered sadly.

Every relationship had been a threat to her success. So back then, and through the years, she'd tied her emotions up as tight as the laces on her skates.

But everything changed when she'd met Derek.

Her face warmed as she watched him down on the basketball court shooting free throws with the players. Only hours before, the same large hands that handled the ball so expertly now had caressed her body as though it was fine sculpture. Did he know that within his hands, he also held her fragile heart?

Natalie shrugged her shoulders. "It was just a name the media came up with. It didn't really mean anything." She opened up her purse and pretended to look for something, hoping that Janet would change the subject.

Just then, the teams and players were announced over the loudspeaker.

"Ladies and gentlemen, we also have tonight with

us a special guest, Derek Lansing, power forward for the New York Skylarks. As many of you know, Derek is an alumnus of Baker's Falls Academy and our fine basketball program. Due to his talent and energy, BFA went the state championships for the first time during his senior year. Right after that, he was a first-round NBA draft pick and his career has skyrocketed ever since. Put your hands together and let's give a warm BFA welcome home to Derek Lansing!"

The crowd stood and erupted in applause. Not only was Derek a celebrity, he was a local hometown hero.

Derek walked out into the center of the court and waved. He appeared pleased, yet seemed to scan the seats, as well. Natalie assumed he was looking for his father. She wondered if he wished Pops was there, watching the town greet him so openly, so happily, while all his father did was slam the door.

The buzzer sounded and the game was about to begin. The players for both teams moved into position on the floor.

That's when Natalie spotted Derek's father standing just under the bleachers at the farthest corner of the court near one of the doors.

Immediately she thought of the promise she'd made to Derek earlier. If Pops was there, they were supposed to leave. She looked at Derek, at Janet, who seemed deeply engrossed in the game, then back at Pops.

Should she tell?

She squinted at the man, and she thought she saw Pops shake his head, as if he'd read her mind. But that was highly unlikely, he was just too far away. Besides, they'd never even met. She wasn't even sure he knew what she looked like to even pick her face out of the large crowd around her.

Still, this was the opportunity she'd hoped for. A second chance for a reunion between Derek and his father. But something told her that the timing wasn't right, and if she interfered now, she could lose Derek forever.

So she turned her eyes away from Pops and back onto Derek, where they belonged.

At halftime Natalie realized Derek's father was gone from under the bleachers. She'd tried to keep tabs on him throughout the game, but it was difficult because she didn't want to call attention to him. Although she didn't know exactly when he'd disappeared, she estimated it was midway through the second quarter.

She felt Janet nudge her arm. "Let's go and meet the guys."

They made their way down the stairs. Music blasted through the loudspeakers. Baker's Falls Academy led their rivals 65–44 and the crowd was pumped with energy.

At courtside Derek put his arm around her and whispered, "Let's get out of here."

She nodded with relief, more than willing to escape the noise that was starting to give her a headache.

He took her hand and led her through another door into an empty auditorium.

"Come on, I want to show you something."

She followed him through another door into an

empty hallway. Her high-heeled shoes clicked on the polished floor.

"Shh… Take those off," he instructed.

She looked at him oddly, but obeyed.

As they walked down a shadowy corridor, Derek began to point out different rooms and she realized he was taking her on a tour of his school. A peek into his past.

Even though no one was around, they spoke in hushed tones, which only accentuated their secretive prowl.

"Room 228. Homeroom. I got my first detention from Mrs. Parker."

"For what?" she asked.

"Being late!" he replied dryly.

"I should have guessed," she said, giggling quietly.

They proceeded down the hall, holding hands, and for a second Natalie imagined what it must have been like to be Derek's girlfriend way back then.

"Room 235. Algebra. The only thing good about that class was the teacher."

She peeked in the glass window. "Oh, was she well qualified?"

"No, but she was well stacked!" he said, cupping his hands under his chest.

She turned around. "Are you trying to make me jealous?" she asked, only half kidding, and attempted to punch him in the arm for his juvenile humor. But he dodged out of the way and ran backward down the hall.

She wanted to throw her shoe at him, but was afraid it would make too much noise.

When she caught up to him, she tugged on his locks. "Any other rooms you want to show me, handsome?"

He nodded, and even in the shadowy light, she could see the devilish glint in his eyes. "As a matter of fact, there is."

They turned down another shorter corridor lined with lockers. Derek stopped at the last door in the hallway.

"Here we are. Room 257."

He pulled out a credit card, bent and started to pick the lock.

She leaned against the wall right next to him and stroked his hair as she watched.

"Hmm… Another one of your talents?"

Derek looked up at her and she raised her eyebrows, tilting her head in mock disapproval.

He winked. "I've got a lot of talents, honey."

She pecked him on the lips. "So I've learned." *And felt.*

He jiggled the handle a little and the door opened.

"Voilà!" he said triumphantly.

She linked her arms around his neck as he pulled her into his arms. "So what room is this?"

"Chemistry," he whispered.

His lips never left hers as they stumbled inside. With one arm clutching her waist, he reached behind them, closed the door and turned the lock.

Natalie flicked her tongue into the small concave at the base of his neck, enjoying the vibrations of Derek's groan against her flesh. She loved pleasing him.

She dragged her fingernails along the smooth ridge

of his collarbone. He pressed his torso to hers and moved slowly against her body. The length of his need for her was deliciously hard against her belly.

The room was dark but she could still see the lab tables scattered around, some of which held scientific equipment. There was a huge chalkboard on one wall with formulas scribbled all over it.

"I used to hate this class," he suddenly blurted.

She broke away from their embrace and stepped back. "Oh, really. Why?"

"Because I was so bad at it," he replied. "It was one of my worst subjects."

She took his hand, turned it upward and kissed his palm.

"Well, it seems like you're acing it now."

He closed his eyes, and she reached up and slipped his suit jacket from his broad shoulders. It fell to the floor with a whoosh that sounded louder than it actually was.

"But if you've forgotten some key facts," she continued, running her hands lightly down his chest, "I'll be happy to refresh your memory."

He began to breathe heavily as she unbuttoned his shirt, planting kisses, keeping her lips buoyant and light, all the way down his chest. Finally she tugged the material out from the waistband of his pants.

Her mouth watered at the sight of the lengthy bulge beneath the blue-jeaned fabric and she started to undo his belt. But before she could, Derek shrugged out of his shirt and seconds later, she was in his arms.

He palmed her face and looked into her eyes.

"I know what chemistry is," he whispered.

Natalie's face went hot at the physical need and caring she saw there in his gray eyes.

He stroked her cheeks lightly with his thumbs, which made her whole body shiver. "It's chemical reactions and bonding and transformation."

She closed her eyes as his lips roamed over hers, sucking and tasting, claiming them as his own. And, oh, how she wanted to be his forever.

"It's you and me," he said between kisses. "It's us."

He broke the embrace and they clung together, both breathing hard. Both needing the other and not wanting to let go.

"I'm falling for you, Natalie." His voice was low and sexy in her ear.

Her eyes widened in surprise and she felt her heart balloon with happiness at his words. And when she looked into his eyes, she saw love there. For her.

She kissed him first this time, their tongues playing games where the only rule was pleasure. Both now drowning in the heat of their desire.

And when she unbuckled his belt and dragged down the zipper, he didn't stop her, but kicked off his shoes instead. Her smile was wicked as she slid his jeans, then his briefs, down to the ground.

His length arrowed forth, hit the cool air. Derek grunted in response and the two bulbs of flesh that hung beneath bobbed.

She stepped back and let him watch as she removed her top and unhooked her bra. He reached for her breasts, eyeing the bare flesh hungrily, but she shook her head and started to take off her skirt.

"Leave it on," he commanded.

She complied, with a smile, and dropped to her knees in front of him. Every part of him was beautiful. But this part, she thought, was absolutely magnificent.

The long core of skin was thick and tight as she closed her lips around him, moving slowly down to encapsulate his entire shaft. And when she began to suck, Derek's guttural moan reverberated in her mouth and she felt her own loins moisten pleasurably.

To have him like this, under her complete control, made her feel intensely powerful. She wanted to love him, needed to love him, in every way possible.

"Natalie," he gasped. His hands cradled her head, guiding her mouth, and she took him in and out, leisurely tonguing him from base to tip. "Oh, girl, what are you doing to me?"

She held on to his thighs. The muscles were tense with pent-up energy, and when they began to shake she knew he was close to release.

He lifted her chin, slipped away and helped her to her feet.

"I need you, Natalie."

His hands slid up under her skirt, removed her underwear and stroked her wet flesh. She moaned. And when he picked her up, she wrapped her legs around his waist and held on tightly.

He walked them over a short distance and she gasped when he pressed her against the cold chalkboard.

Kneading her buttocks, he stepped away slightly and

bent his head to one breast. She cried out as he nibbled on the supple, stiff tip. Her thighs pulsed and throbbed and she clamped them around his waist even harder.

"Derek?" she moaned, watching him suck on her nipples. "Why did you act like we were a couple when we really weren't?"

He lifted his mouth from her skin and palmed her face. His steel-gray eyes glazed with need. "Wishful thinking, I guess."

She gyrated her inner lips, allowing them to slide and mesh and mold against his long, hard core. It felt like a rod of fire against her wet flesh. "You don't have to wish anymore."

"I know," he moaned, and his hands lifted her up again.

And at that moment, he slammed into her.

Chalk dust flew into the air as he penetrated and released, coveted and gave, again and again. Their lips tasted and their tongues clashed in each other's mouths. Her spirit soared higher as her hands urged him on, faster and faster, until her whole body shuddered with pleasure and she covered her screams by biting his neck.

The swell.

The crest.

His exuberant release.

Her tears of joy.

Chapter 9

"Woman," Derek gasped against her shoulder. "That was some chemistry lesson."

Natalie laughed, twirling one of his locks around her finger. "Just wait till I show you what I have in store for home economics," she teased.

A couple of seconds later red lights slashed into the room and danced on the walls, followed by the chaotic whine of sirens.

Her heart dropped when she suddenly realized with horror that the chemistry room was at the front of the school building. Even though it was already dark outside, what if someone had walked by and seen them making love and had called the cops?

They dressed quickly and Derek looked out the window.

"There's an ambulance and a couple of squad cars," he reported. "We better see what's going on."

Natalie nodded and held on to the lab table to steady her wobbly legs as she slipped into her shoes.

"I hope nothing happened to any of the players," she said, recalling past news reports of young athletes being killed by a sudden heart attack.

As they rushed through the darkened hallways, Natalie couldn't help but feel disappointed that their evening had been interrupted. On the other hand, she hoped no one was seriously hurt.

When they got outside, the air was cool and stars dotted the night sky. But the peaceful atmosphere was shattered by the fragmented shouts of police officers, the whirring red lights, the patches of crowds gathering and pointing and the sense that something was very, very wrong.

She heard the slap of heavy footsteps running toward them.

"Derek!" Wes shouted. When he caught up to the couple, he was breathing hard.

"You gotta come with me." Wes coughed hard and spat on the ground. "Right now."

Derek grabbed him by the arm. "What's wrong?" he demanded.

"It's Pops," Wes said, heaving in large, desperate breaths. "They found him on the ground by his car."

The blood in Natalie's veins turned icy. "Oh, God."

Derek's head snapped up and he released his brother's arm.

He looked around in confusion. "Here?" he asked

with a combination of surprise and suspicion in his voice. “In this parking lot?”

Wes nodded, a little guiltily. “Yeah. He was at the game the whole time.”

Natalie gasped in surprise, then quickly covered her mouth.

Derek whirled toward her, his eyes clouded with pain. “Did you know about this?”

She swallowed back the huge lump in her throat. “I—I saw him near the bleachers. I meant to tell you at halftime, but he was gone.”

Both men widened their eyes at her confession.

“How is he?” Natalie asked, voicing the question Derek should have asked right away. Was his heart so hardened against his father that he no longer cared about his well-being?

A second later she rebuked herself because she knew that Derek did care about his father. He cared a lot. The man was just in shock. That’s why he was reacting this way.

“I don’t know,” Wes responded, pointing toward the ambulance. “The paramedics are working on stabilizing him before they transport him to the hospital.”

Derek seemed not to hear their conversation. “Why didn’t you tell me he was here?” he asked, posing the question to both of them, although she knew it was meant mainly for her. She’d made a promise and had broken it.

Wes glanced back at the ambulance and swore when he saw the medics shutting the doors.

“None of that matters now,” Wes barked. His voice

was gruff and he seemed on the edge of tears. "They're about to leave and take him to the hospital. We need to go! Now."

Natalie saw Janet standing beside the ambulance, motioning frantically to the group.

Wes turned to Natalie. "Can you take Janet back home? The Red Hat ladies will be arriving back from the play shortly and she needs to be there to greet them. Derek and I will follow the ambulance to the hospital in my truck."

Natalie nodded. "Of course, I'll do anything I can to help."

Derek wouldn't even look at her when, for the second time that day, he handed her the keys to his car. Without saying goodbye, the two men took off toward Wes's truck, got in and sped off.

She quickly located the Jeep, got in and turned the key in the ignition, wondering if she should have asked Derek if he wanted her to meet him at the hospital after she dropped Janet off at Belle Amour.

Her heart sank when she realized that right now he probably didn't want to deal with anything or anyone—especially her. And after what she'd done to him tonight, she doubted he ever would.

No, not like this.

For the first time in years Derek was alone with his dad.

He pulled a chair up alongside the hospital bed and felt like he was watching a nightmare. Tubes and wires were everywhere. A heart monitor beeped out a steady rhythm, while the man who'd raised him lay there in a medically induced sleep. His father had been knocked unconscious by the fall and until the results of testing came back, they wouldn't know the extent of his injuries.

Derek's eyes welled with tears. "Don't die on me, Pops."

They'd been an every-Sunday-morning churchgoing family, but Derek had never put much stock in faith when he was growing up.

"Lord," he prayed, "I could sure use some help now."

He glanced over at the door. Wes had just left to find the doctor for an update and to make some phone calls. He'd be back shortly.

Derek didn't have much time.

Tentatively he touched his father's hand, veined with age. It should have been easy for Derek to say the things he'd waited years to express. But when he opened his mouth, no words came.

At that moment he felt as frail and as helpless as his father looked.

He stared at the white walls, unsure of what to do next.

The anger he felt earlier, knowing that his father had been at the game and had chosen to ignore him, was simply gone. And in its place, the would-have, should-have pang of regret moved in.

He buried his face in his hands, wishing he'd gone after his father yesterday morning at his office and confronted him, instead of running away from the conflict, just as he'd done so many years ago.

He'd accepted the slammed door. The months, then years of estrangement. Time with his father that he could never get back.

And now, it could be too late.

Shame burned through the tears in his eyes.

The last words he'd spoken to his dad, on the day he told him of his decision to skip college and play pro basketball instead, were so cruel, so cutting.

You're just a stupid janitor who walks around with a mop and bucket. What do you know about multimillion-dollar deals?

He winced at the memory of their argument.

"I was the one who was stupid," he whispered, squeezing his father's hand gently. "You knew the money wouldn't make me happy, didn't you, Pops?"

Suddenly the door opened and he quickly wiped his eyes.

"What did the doctor say?" he asked without turning around.

Silence.

He swiveled in his chair.

Natalie.

Despite the combination of emotions he was feeling at the moment, his heart did a somersault at the sight of her.

She'd changed into jeans and a loose-fitting T-shirt, and wore no makeup, yet to him she looked gorgeous.

She stood with a morose expression on her face, her hands clasped loosely in front of her. It was as if she was waiting for him to invite her in, and she was unsure if she was welcome.

And at that moment he knew he loved her. When he'd least expected it, she'd become a part of him. A part of his world.

But more than that, she'd known he would need her, even if he refused to acknowledge it, and she'd come.

He stood, the chair scraping against the tile floor, went to her and engulfed her in his arms. He kissed the top of her head. Her shiny black hair still smelled like apricots and he longed to bury his face in it.

"I'm so sorry, Derek." Natalie cried against his chest. "If only I'd told you your father was at the game."

"Shh..." he soothed, wishing she hadn't even brought it up. They'd had a deal. She'd made a promise to him. A promise she hadn't kept. He'd started to trust her; now he wasn't so sure that he could. His heart and his mind was in such a mix of emotions, he didn't know what to do.

Why did it always seem like heartbreak was the backside of happiness?

Derek shrugged out of their embrace, not because he didn't enjoy holding her, but he just wanted to get away. From her. From everyone. But Pops needed him.

Derek walked over to the bedside and stared at the motionless figure. At least he hoped he did, even though he couldn't tell him now.

"What happened?" Natalie asked quietly.

Derek touched his father's hand. "He collapsed getting into his car. They don't know how serious his head injuries might be."

Natalie placed a hand over her mouth. "How long was he lying there?"

He turned toward her. "They don't know," he responded. "I was hoping you could tell me."

Her eyes widened with confusion. "How would I know, Derek? I was with you the entire time." She paused, and her cheeks were spotted with color. "Don't you remember?"

He'd never forget. She'd nearly done him in with her lovemaking skills, and he was looking forward to being with her again—both in and out of bed. But at this point, even though he loved her, he didn't know what the future held for either of them.

"Of course I do. But you saw him at the game, not me. Don't *you* remember?"

Her mouth dropped open in shock at his tone, but at that moment he didn't care if his voice or his words sounded harsh. He needed answers, not secrets, and he needed them now.

He gave her a pointed look. "When was the last time you saw him?"

She fiddled with one of her earrings nervously. "I think he left sometime in the second quarter." She paused and thought some more. "Yes, I know he wasn't there at halftime," she said with a definitive nod.

"Oh, no." Derek plopped down in the chair next to the bed. Even though he was in great physical condition for an athlete his age, his body felt like it weighed a ton. "That's longer than I thought."

She sat in the chair next to him, a worried look on her face. "Why? What's wrong?"

"So if he left at halftime and that's when he fell, Pops wasn't spotted till the game was nearly over. That means he was lying there with no help for a long time. I learned today that he also has epilepsy, which means he may have been having a seizure that caused him to fall."

Natalie gasped. "That's terrible."

Avoiding her eyes, he got up and stared at the heart monitor, although he had no idea how to read it. The blips and beeps were as mysterious as the reasons why Wes had neglected to tell Derek about their father's medical condition. His brother should have told him right away instead of keeping it a secret.

Derek clenched his jaw to stem his anger.

If only I had known.

"If he did have a seizure, do the doctors know what triggered it?" Natalie asked.

Derek reluctantly turned away from the monitor and shook his head, even though he knew what had caused it.

It was him.

Clearly, Derek's visit had upset his father. So if anyone was to blame, he was.

"They don't know if there's been any damage to his brain," Derek said, gulping back a sob.

He pulled Natalie to him, not caring now if she saw the tears in his eyes. All he wanted was to feel her warm body cradled in his arms.

"Oh, God, I should have listened to Wes. I never should have gone to his office today."

Natalie stood back and grasped his shoulders. Her grip was tight, but loving.

"Don't say that, Derek," she said sternly. "You did what you thought was right."

Derek hung his head. “No. He didn’t even want to see me. I should have waited. And now he’ll never know that I—”

Natalie placed her palm against his cheek. “What? That you love him? Care about him? You can still tell him, Derek.”

He shrank away from her touch. “Don’t you understand that I can’t do that?” he snapped. “I just can’t!”

He knew Natalie had the best intentions. She was trying to be efficient and to help reunite the Lansing men. But she still didn’t get it.

He strode over to the window and balled his hands up on the sill. He’d never felt so angry. So lost and alone. And something else he would never admit to anyone—scared.

The truth was that he wasn’t ready to talk to his father. And obviously, his father felt the same. Derek knew he couldn’t handle any more rejection. Maybe his father couldn’t, either.

They were at a stalemate.

But it didn’t matter now.

Not with his father lying in a hospital bed, unable to speak, while his older son stood by, unable to help or to do anything at all.

Besides, Derek knew that his father wouldn’t believe he cared about anything but himself. And back then, he would have been right.

But now? Everything had changed.

He looked down at the street below where nothing moved in the early morning darkness.

He stared at the puddles dotting the glistening sidewalks. When had it rained? He remembered how his dad loved to sit on the porch during a thunderstorm. He'd always say that after a good rain, the world looked and smelled as "new as when the Lord first created it."

Tears sprung to his eyes again. When this was all over, would his father ever be able to smell the fresh air, feel the raindrops or hear his apologies?

"Derek, it's okay."

He felt Natalie's hand trail down his back. It amazed him how the simplest touch from her inflamed his desires, even now, when he couldn't do a damn thing about it.

"I'm sorry," she said. Her voice was soft and caring. "I didn't mean to push you. You don't have to do or say anything you don't feel completely comfortable with."

Her soft voice was the perfect backdrop for a genuine apology, but it rang hollow in his ears. He didn't want to listen to anything but the sound of his father waking up and speaking.

"He's so medicated that he can't hear what I say anyway," he muttered, still facing the window.

"I don't know," Natalie said. "He may hear more than we think he can."

His heart lifted at the hopeful tone in her voice. But then it suddenly occurred to Derek that his father and Natalie had a lot in common. They were both dreamers.

Natalie dreamed of princes and castles and true love.

His father dreamed of moving up in the world and restored love.

Derek, on the other hand, was a realist. He knew life was about dollars and cents, points and popularity.

Love just got in the way of things. Even though deep in his heart, he wished that wasn't true.

Natalie touched his arm, interrupting his thoughts. "Can I give you some advice, as your life coach?"

He turned toward her. "Do I have the right to refuse?" he said, cracking a reluctant smile.

She folded her arms, and he could tell she was annoyed. "No. You're paying me to give you advice, so I'm going to give it!"

"Let me guess. You're going to tell me to keep my chin up because everything will work out in the end," he mocked.

"I wish I could say that it will." She took a deep breath. "But on the contrary. My advice is to stay in the moment. No matter how difficult or dark it may be."

Derek stared at her, then narrowed his eyes. "'Stay in the moment'?" he repeated. "Are you kidding me?"

He pointed to his father, struggling to keep his voice low. "Look at him! Are you saying that you expect me to accept what's going on here?"

He jabbed his thumb into his chest. "I'm the reason he's laying there, Natalie! I'm the cause!" he stressed.

Natalie shook her head. "No, I'm not saying you have to accept this, and I refuse to believe that anyone is to blame for what's happened.

"But staying in the moment can help you stop focusing on the past and pointing fingers, mostly at yourself," she added calmly.

"That's where you're wrong," he insisted. "My past and my mistakes are what got my father here in the first place. No amount of your positive-thinking psychobabble is going to change that."

At his words her face contorted and she backed away, almost imperceptibly. Although he knew he should apologize, all he could think about was his pain and his guilt.

Still he reached out to touch her, but she took another step back, firmly establishing the imaginary wall between them.

"Feeling sorry for yourself won't change things, either, Derek," she said quietly.

His heart seized up in his chest. Her words were true, but he would never admit it. He had too much pride.

But he loved her and wanted to shield her from any further emotional pain. Especially the kind caused by him.

"I just want to be alone," he said evenly.

Her eyes blinked rapidly and he hoped she wouldn't cry.

"Fine. I'll call a cab back to Belle Amour."

Without another word, she turned and walked to the door, opened it and almost collided with Wes.

"Whoa! Where are you going in such a hurry?" he asked.

Natalie glanced back at Derek, her eyes dark with hurt.

"Home," she responded icily. "Where I belong."

Her words splintered through Derek's brain and panic raced through him. Was she going back to New York? And why did even the possibility that she would go frighten him? It made him want to fight to keep her near, but perhaps it was better this way.

She was right to be cautious about any sort of relationship with him. The pull of the basketball court, the money and everything that went along with being a sports superstar was still very strong. He just wasn't sure he could give all that up for anything or anyone.

He'd taken a huge risk already. He'd never before had the courage to talk about his feelings, and telling Natalie that he was falling in love with her was a huge step in the right direction for him. But even though their lovemaking was incredible, she'd never told him how she felt about him, and that hurt.

Did Natalie love him? If she did, then why had she broken her promise to tell him if she saw Pops at the game? Although he knew none of this was truly her fault, his burgeoning trust in her had taken a huge hit. Watching her walk out, he hoped it wasn't the last time he would see her.

Without looking at Wes, he pulled out the visitor's chair, sat and buried his face in his hands.

Wes shut the door and walked over to him.

"What's wrong with you, man?"

Derek ran his fingers down his face, the whiskers on his unshaven face were rough. He felt like a bum.

"Nothing, okay?"

Wes crossed over to the other side of the bed, eyeing him skeptically. "Whatever's going on with Pops, don't take it out on your woman."

Derek blew out a harsh breath. "She's *not* my woman." Although he desperately wanted her to be.

Wes raised his eyebrows. "You said she was your girlfriend, and the two of you looked mighty cozy yesterday."

"You just thought she was," he replied, shaking his head emphatically and at the same time feeling a little dishonest. Relationship labels aside, his heart knew the truth.

"Who is she then?" Wes asked.

"A life coach. Just as she said. My manager hired her to help me get my life together."

"What's wrong with it?" Wes's eyes crinkled at the corners, as if he was about to laugh, but he didn't. "Looks to me like you have it all. Money, fame, fortune."

Derek watched his father's chest rise and fall with the help of the respirator. "You know, Wes, life's not all about the Benjamins."

Wes cocked his eyebrow again. "I've always been down with that. But you?" He shook his head. "No offense, bro. But money was all you cared about."

"Used to care about," Derek corrected.

Until I met Natalie.

To be fair, he'd been disenchanted with his lifestyle for quite a while. He couldn't pinpoint exactly what had triggered his unhappiness, but it was a slow, silent death.

The awareness that he needed to change hadn't happened overnight, either.

His need for popularity was both a cure for his love-starved heart and poison for his soul. The worst part?

Not knowing if people liked you for who you were, rather than what you could do for them.

And the money? Ah…those paper-thin, printed slivers of green presidents and their hard-plastic, colorful cousins were always vying for his attention.

It was a good thing he was a saver, not a spender. His only real vice was his plane and a bottle of Dom or vintage wine every once in a while.

His eyes slid shut and he immediately thought of Natalie. Her jet-black hair, her long legs and the curves that drove him mad with desire. He'd only known her for a little while, yet he'd waited a lifetime for her.

She was the catalyst. The reason he wanted to finally put the effort into changing his image. Manufactured as it was, he was ashamed to admit he'd bought into it, too. It was just easier that way. He avoided the inevitable conflicts with his manager, the owner of the Skylarks and the press. And in a way, he was protected. His image was a shield. No one could get close.

What would his fans think if they found out he was a really nice guy and not the player his manager had made him out to be all these years?

Changing wouldn't be easy and it would be even harder without Natalie at his side.

It was she who brought to the surface the thoughts he'd been trying to squash for years.

What was he doing with his life?

Who was he helping, besides himself, with all his millions?

He felt a hand on his shoulder.

"Hey, wake up!" Wes said, shaking him a little.

With a yawn, he rubbed his eyes open. "I'm up."

"I know you haven't gotten a lot of sleep in the past twenty-four hours," Wes said. "Why don't you go home and get some rest? I'll stay with Pops for the rest of the night."

Derek shook his head stubbornly. "I want to be here when the doctor comes in."

Wes leaned against the windowsill. "The head nurse told me he had an emergency surgery. It'll be a while."

Derek grunted out his frustration. He understood that hospitals were busy places. That everybody's blood was the same color, no matter how much or how little money you had in your pocket.

Yet he still opened his mouth and almost blurted, "Doesn't that doctor know who I am?"

But his jaw snapped closed, as shame rushed through him, knowing Pops wouldn't have liked him to throw his status around. Use it to gain special attention or privileges. No matter how sick he was.

When he and Wes were growing up, Pops had taught them to be humble and thankful because one day they would both realize all they really needed was—

Family.

Derek hitched in a breath and stared at his dad, then at Wes. And his heart swelled with a strange and bittersweet kind of happiness.

Here they were again. Reunited. The three Lansing men.

Could they ever be a family again?

He eyed Pops again with deep concern.

It wasn't the best of circumstances. In fact, it was

the worst possible circumstances. But those were the cards the three men had been dealt.

Still, they were together again. And right now, that was all that mattered.

Wes coughed, interrupting his thoughts. "When is the last time you've eaten?"

Derek yawned. "I honestly don't remember." Between worrying about his relationship with Natalie and his dad's precarious health, food was the last thing on his mind.

Wes frowned. "Well, if you won't go home and sleep, let's go down to the cafeteria. I don't know what they're serving at—" he checked his watch "—3:00 a.m., but I'm betting the coffee is hot."

Derek nodded toward the door. "You go on and bring me one back. I'll stay here with Pops."

After Wes left, the room seemed to breathe silence, like a ferocious monster bent on destroying everything in its path. Derek wallowed in it, his eyes never leaving his father, as he tried to scrape past the desolate helplessness he felt at that moment.

Finally he stood and leaned over the bed. He smoothed the wrinkles from the thick blanket covering his father and gently tugged it closer, just under his chin. If his father woke up, he didn't want him to wake up cold…or alone.

Even though Pops probably didn't want him there, Derek was glad he'd stayed. At the same time, he also didn't want to go back to Belle Amour and face Natalie. Deep down, he just couldn't bear it if she wasn't there waiting for him.

Chapter 10

Natalie tiptoed up the stairs to the bridal suite, being careful not to make any noise, lest she awaken the Red Hat Society ladies all nestled in their beds. They were a lively bunch, and right now, she wished she was one of them, and that the only thing on her agenda was to enjoy Shakespeare and pleasantries with friends.

Instead she was faced with a decision.

Should she stay in Baker's Falls with Derek or should she hightail it back to New York?

Bending, she dragged her suitcase from under the bed, as if the very action of doing so would provide the answer. It was heavy—she always overpacked—plus she was dead tired. She had just enough energy to throw in the rest of her clothes before collapsing on the mattress.

She passed her fingers through her hair, messing it up, but she didn't care. It was after 3:00 a.m., far past the time of accountability from a makeup perspective.

But more importantly, Derek was at the hospital, where his father was in serious condition, and she was lying here actually contemplating leaving him.

A sudden wind huffed through the open window, as if to scold her.

How could you? You love him! it seemed to accuse.

Her breath caught in her throat. Did she love Derek?

She watched the curtains billow out and then collapse against the sill. At this point, she didn't know what she felt, and that's what bothered her the most.

When she was a psychologist, or even now as a life coach, she'd helped guide her patients beyond their painful pasts or life-changing circumstances, such as death or divorce, so that they could identify and accept their feelings and come to their own conclusions.

The answers they sought were always there. They simply had to learn to listen to their hearts.

A second gust of wind blew into the room, bringing with it an early morning chill. She shivered, hugging her knees to her chest.

Maybe it was time for her to take her own advice.

She turned and looked at the mahogany bureau where earlier that evening, which seemed like a lifetime ago, she'd had the pleasure of watching Derek getting dressed for the basketball game.

Following an afternoon of intense lovemaking, it would seem as if the act of getting dressed would be just an ordinary, dull activity.

But it wasn't and her mouth watered as her body reacted physically to the images that settled comfortably in her mind.

She hugged her knees tighter against the delicious hum in her lower belly, recalling how she'd felt a bit like a voyeur. The way Derek had pulled on his boxers over his rock-hard length had been downright scandalous.

Yes, she desired him deeply. She'd never wanted a man so completely, so endlessly, as Derek. But when she peeled back the layers of pure lust, she discovered that when she was away from him, her heart ached.

As soon as he was out of her sight, she missed him. The moment his body slipped from hers, she wanted him again. The mere thought of never seeing him again left her with a deep sense of isolation that she didn't understand.

A lone cricket chirped and the wind was now a gentle breeze. Although she was rarely up this early, unless she couldn't sleep, she loved this time of morning. The utter stillness, that hush of suspended activity and thoughts, was like a blank canvas where anything was possible. And loving Derek, even having a steady relationship with him, was not out of the bounds of her imagination.

It was a real possibility.

In the quiet of the night, her fears of their relationship not working out because of their hectic work and travel schedules? Gone.

In the depths of her heart, she knew that holding back her feelings from Derek wasn't doing either of them any good. There was too much at risk, and still far too much to discover, both individually and as a couple.

She glanced over at the door and wondered if Derek would be back soon. The way she was feeling right now, she'd likely rush at him as soon as he walked in and confess her love for him.

Before she lost her nerve.

Before it was too late.

Tears sprang to her eyes as she thought about her parents. They'd been gone a little more than eleven years now, yet the guilt was still fresh. When she was older and actually had the ability to express her feelings, she hadn't. She was always afraid it was too late, that her words would never cover up the pain she knew she'd caused them. So, consequently, they'd never known how much she'd loved and appreciated them.

She couldn't let the same thing happen with Derek.

But how to close the gap that had widened between them? He'd pushed her away. She knew she'd broken his trust, and maybe even his heart. She was afraid that whatever she did would only make things worse.

Oh, how she wished she were a little girl again. When life was easier and her thoughts were of colorful storybooks, glittery skating outfits and a handsome prince.

She'd never imagined that her prince would be someone who was not only handsome, but as talented and kind as Derek.

"With a basketball in his hands, instead of the reins of a brilliant white horse and a red rose between his teeth," she murmured to herself, her lips curving into a smile.

Yawning, she released her arms from around her

knees and stretched like a cat. The bed had been turned down and she could easily get underneath the covers and go to sleep.

Suddenly she sat straight, an idea formulating in her mind.

Why not? she thought.

She quickly zipped up her suitcase and set it near the door. After washing her face and brushing her teeth, she carefully removed the huge bedspread. She tucked a couple of pillows under her arms and proceeded to half carry, half drag the bedspread up the narrow stairs to the Turret Room, feeling a little like a child and a lot adventurous.

After cranking open the windows, she laid the bedspread and pillows carefully on the wide planks of the floor, as close to the baseboard as possible.

She removed her clothes, folded the bedspread into a makeshift sleeping bag and got in. From her vantage point, she could see the moon sitting high among the stars.

The Turret Room was the closest she'd ever come to being able to sleep nude under the stars and she was going to take full advantage of it. It was totally private and far more comfortable than camping. Plus, no mosquito bites and no wild animals.

The breeze, scented with daffodils, curled around her like an invisible blanket, awakening her senses. She stared up at the stars as a deep sense of peace enveloped her, and she was glad to have it.

Her job as a life coach was devoted to helping people empower themselves and achieve their goals. She took her responsibilities very seriously and consequently was constantly under an enormous amount of stress and pressure. She was always organizing someone, going somewhere and doing something.

It was nice to just lie here and be a woman. Natalie snuggled deep into the bedspread, closed her eyes and drifted off to sleep.

It could have been a few minutes or an hour later when she was roused from her slumber by a creak on the stairwell. In an instant she knew that Derek was there. She bit her lip and froze, and thought about pretending she was still asleep. But his imposing presence was like a magnetic force that would not be ignored.

Yet she did not turn to face him as tears formed beneath her closed eyelids.

"You came back," she whispered.

His sigh was deep and troubled.

"You're still here." His voice was low, yet seemed to fill the space between them. "I saw your suitcase by the door and I thought..."

She rolled to face him then, being careful not to reveal her nakedness.

He dropped to his knees beside her, and his voice broke.

"I got scared."

The brutal honesty of those three words pierced her heart and confused her mind.

Could he really want her to stay with him?

"I couldn't leave." She took a deep breath for courage, yet her voice was still barely above a whisper. "Not until you and your father are reunited."

She propped herself up on one elbow and stared into his eyes. "The way *you* want to be."

He sank back on his heels and bowed his head, locks swooshing over his face. She watched with interest as his chest expanded and contracted, as if it was weighing and measuring every thought running through his mind.

Even his breathing fascinated her.

Finally he lifted his head and his eyes sealed with hers.

"What I want is you. By my side."

She took in a sharp breath, not bothering to wipe away the tears that fell from her eyes. Warmth pooled in her belly, along with the fear she thought she'd defeated in the early morning calm.

Wasn't this what she wanted to hear? Yet his words made her hopes of being with him all too real.

She knew getting involved with Derek on a permanent basis could be a big mistake. Or it could be the best decision she ever made in her life.

His words. Did he really mean them? He'd been through a very traumatic experience and she knew that sometimes when people went through something like that they said things they regretted.

The silence in the little room only magnified the boldness of their gaze, wired together by something more than desire and threatening her resolve to further question his motives.

Unsure of how to respond, she closed her eyes and shivered as Derek's fingertips lightly brushed against her eyelashes.

"You look so beautiful in the moonlight. Even your tears sparkle."

Still propped up on one elbow, Natalie kept her eyes closed, regretting he'd seen her cry, and choked out a tiny laugh. "You're so exhausted you can't see straight."

He ran his thumb over the little indent in her chin, oddly one of the most sensitive parts of her face. His tender movements sent pebbles of sensation zinging through her body and she stifled the urge to moan.

"I can see fine, and I'd never tire of looking at you."

And then his mouth suddenly closed over hers, and she did moan as his tongue gently invited and boldly tasted the unspoken passion for him that she could no longer ignore.

Weak with desire, her elbow gave out and she sank back onto the floor as Derek stretched out alongside her and at the same time gathered her into his muscular arms.

The lion and his lioness.

They breathed life into each other with every precious kiss. His long locks cocooned her face in a jungle of steamy darkness and when she brushed his hair aside, he caught her wrist and nibbled it.

The thick bedspread wrapped around her could not repel the warmth of his hard body upon hers. In fact, it made her even hotter, and she yearned to throw the covers off and feel him.

Yet he did not ask to see her and her ego wondered why, although her concern was quickly overshadowed by merely succumbing to his rapt attention.

When he finally lifted his lips from hers, she clasped

her arms around his neck and tried to pull him back. She didn't want the kisses to stop.

But he resisted and she whimpered, letting her arms fall to the side in defeat.

"Open your eyes," he commanded.

She hesitated a bit, not really knowing why she was afraid, but she was.

She didn't want the dream to end.

He spoke again. "Look at me, Natalie."

Finally she complied and when she opened her eyes, her heart plummeted at what she saw.

His eyes had lost the steely harshness she'd noted earlier at the hospital. They were softer now. Sadder.

"I have to tell you something."

His breath was warm upon her cheek and she blinked in the seriousness of his gaze.

She shook her head. "Let me go first."

He reeled back a little, as if surprised, and nodded.

She took a deep breath and plunged in, before she lost her nerve. "When I was a little girl, I wasn't the nicest person."

His forehead crinkled with concern. "What do you mean?"

"I was distant. Afraid." She frowned and paused. "And a spoiled brat."

His low chuckle vibrated like a plucked string through her body. "I have a hard time believing that about you."

"But it's true," she insisted.

She had to make him understand.

"Even though my parents were doctors and they

spent most of their time at the hospital, their whole lives revolved around me. Deep down, I knew it and yet I was angry that they were never around. Especially when I started really getting into ice skating."

"They must have been so proud of you," he commented.

"Yes," she replied, nodding. "But I didn't realize it then. All I knew was at the most important times in my life, they weren't there."

Her mind clouded with memories of taking the subway alone to countless early morning skating sessions and traveling to different skating competitions with her coach at her side instead of her parents because they were always "on call."

Back then, she hadn't been afraid of flying.

He stroked one finger down her cheek, rousing her from her memories. "That must have been so hard for you."

Her eyes flapped open. "It was and, unfortunately, I made sure they knew it."

"How?" he asked.

She forced herself to meet his gaze. "By withholding the only thing they wanted from me." Her voice caught in her throat. "My love."

He patted her arm, as if she were a child. "I'm sure they knew how you felt about them."

"No. I don't think so," she replied, shaking her head. "I never told them and I was so hateful sometimes. When we did have a rare opportunity to do something as a family, I practically ignored them. And when they went back to the hospital, I craved their attention."

"Sounds like a case of normal teenage rebellion to me."

Natalie nodded. "There was definitely some of that. I wasn't afraid of flying then."

Derek squeezed her hand. "What do you mean?"

"On their way to surprise me at one of my skating competitions, my parents died in a freak plane accident. I never skated again."

He gathered her into his arms. "Oh, honey, I'm so sorry."

"I miss them, Derek," she cried. "I always miss them, but for some reason, I miss them more right now than I ever have before."

Derek held her tighter. "I understand."

The musky scent of his cologne wafted into her nose and she wanted to burrow her head against his chest. Yet the simplicity of his response caused her to pull away. She wanted more than courteous platitudes; she wanted an explanation.

"How could you possibly understand?"

There was torment in his eyes and she knew that the decision to open up to her was not an easy one. His world had been turned upside down and the trust beginning to grow between them had been shaken.

In the Turret Room, and in that moment, it was as if they were two inanimate figures encapsulated in a snow globe. The glitter of what was right and true before the unfortunate events of the evening swirled around them. When the glitter finally settled, nothing would be the same.

"I haven't seen my mom since I was thirteen years

old." He shrugged in an offhand manner. "I don't know if she is dead or alive."

If one overheard their conversation, one might think Derek didn't care one way or another, but she sensed that he did.

"Don't you want to find out?" She imagined with his financial resources that he could hire a private detective to find his mother, unearth the sordid details, and then he could choose what to do with any information.

She was surprised when he shook his head. "Sometimes it's better to leave things alone and unanswered." He looked away, but not before she saw the pain etched in his face. "I don't want my dad's heart to break all over again, especially now."

Her heart went out to him, and she wished she'd never pulled away from his embrace.

Losing a mother at any age is very traumatic, but even more so during adolescence, when teens start to discover and define their independence. A mother served as an immovable rock in an unstable and often cruel world. Sacrificing her needs and loving even when it hurt, even when it seemed impossible.

Suddenly in the midst of Derek's despair her long-held belief that her parents never loved her shattered. In her soul, she knew they'd loved her when she was a bratty teen and even now, as the ice around her heart was beginning to melt.

"That's why it's so important to make things right with your dad. You may never have another chance."

A guttural sigh escaped his lips. "I know. I realized

that tonight sitting with him. Watching him sleep. Wondering what I would do if he never woke up."

"Don't you see, Derek? It's not too late for you."

He shifted and sat up, his long arms wrapped around his knees.

"What is it?" Natalie asked, putting her hand on his knees. His eyes flicked down at her touch. "Did you guys meet with the doctor?"

Derek nodded. "He said when swelling went down enough, he'd toggle back on the sedation medication and start to wake him up."

She clapped her hands together. "That's wonderful news! He'll be awake soon."

"What do you think will happen then?" His voice had lost its hard edge as hope started to creep in. "You saw what happened the last time he laid his eyes on me."

She didn't respond, didn't want to recall the resentment between father and son, the years of indifference exposed with all its ugliness in a few minutes. She'd been a witness to emotional pain that had nothing to do with her, yet now she was entwined in it.

"He would have thrown me out of his office if he could."

She looked at him, ignoring the doubt in his eyes, preferring to deal in truth.

"You didn't give him a chance."

He stared at her. "What did you expect me to do, Natalie?"

"Talk to him, Derek," she said gently. "Just talk to him."

His biceps curled around his knees even tighter. "You can't talk to a closed door," he muttered stubbornly.

"Or a closed heart," she replied as she sat up, clutching the blanket around her own bent knees.

Derek dropped his arms. "But what if he opens his eyes and he sees the same person? What then?" he asked, sounding defeated.

"You have to show him you're different. That you're trying."

"But how?" he challenged.

"Just by being there."

Derek nodded and fell silent, seeming to weigh and measure her words. Her advice was matter-of-fact, but his entire future lay within those words.

A bird chirped nearby, punctuating the lush stillness of the room.

His head tilted up. "It's almost sunrise."

She lay back down and turned her head toward the window.

The sky had begun to shed its stars for a faint hue of pink, yet there was still a little night left. A little more time for the two of them.

She opened the blanket, exposing her nakedness, inviting him into her need.

He stared longingly at her body, and her skin tingled and puckered in all the places his eyes roamed.

"Come on in, where it's warm."

Where I can pretend you will be forever.

Could he feel her love for him in her eyes?

He slipped off his shoes, then his socks, and she marveled silently at the enormity of his muscled feet. Wordlessly, he lifted his shirt up and over his arms, then slid his pants and underwear off. His desire for her reared forth, blameless and beautiful.

He lay beside her and nestled his face in her neck, molded his body to hers, as the emotions he'd held in all day finally found a place for release.

She hardly knew Derek, but was content with discovering him, as he was discovering himself. So she stroked his hair, the curves of her neck wet, and hoped her gentle touch would speak the words she longed to say.

You belong here.

With me.

At least for now.

And she held him as night turned into day.

Chapter 11

Late that morning, Natalie woke to the wail of sirens and no sign of Derek. Panic laced through her as she threw off the blanket and stood at the window. A police car sped past Belle Amour and stopped at another home a few doors down the street.

She sighed in relief, grateful for the wake-up call and that Derek wasn't hurt. She looked around the room and noticed his clothes were gone. Where was he?

Although they hadn't made love last night, the intimacy that transpired between them was just as magical. The sunlight flowed through the windows and heated her face, while at the same time mocked her desire to grasp and hold on to everything that had happened between them. To keep him near her.

Yet she knew Derek was like a dream that you wake

up from and then try to sink back into its velvety pleasure, but it always escapes. Making you wonder if you even dreamed at all.

That was Derek. Sleek and sexy and independent. Always driving toward the goal, which most likely did not include her. She would do well to remember that.

Still, she quickly gathered everything and went down the stairs, hoping to catch him by surprise in the shower. But he wasn't there, so she bathed alone and made a decision: she would leave for New York today. She was confident that Derek would take the next step and reconcile with his father. However she wasn't so confident in her ability to prevent herself from falling deeper in love with Derek. So, she had to leave.

After dressing, she grabbed her suitcase and went downstairs.

She found Janet in the parlor, clipping coupons.

"Good morning! I'm late," she lamented, waving one in her hand. "New ones come out in tomorrow's paper and I still haven't clipped the ones from last week." She chuckled. "Guess I could use some of your time management advice."

"As organized as I am, I never had the patience," Natalie commented, entering the room.

"Wes and I save a ton of money every month when we use coupons. I clip and he pulls the carts and stocks everything. It's a team effort."

Natalie smiled. "Are they at the hospital?"

Janet nodded. "Wes got back around 6:00 a.m. He slept a few hours, showered, and they both left here about nine-thirty in the truck. Did the sirens wake you?"

Natalie nodded and sat on a Victorian settee, likely the same one Derek had slept on the first night they'd arrived.

"I'm so sorry. The Powells. They must have a faulty alarm system that goes haywire every couple of days. Are you hungry?"

Natalie started to decline the offer, but she was starving. "Yes, but I know I'm way past breakfast, so I don't want you to go to any trouble."

Janet slipped a wad of coupons into a purple appendix folder. "No trouble at all. I've got fresh-baked biscuits and the coffee is fresh-brewed."

"But it's almost time for lunch," Natalie protested. "I don't want to keep you."

"Thankfully my red-hatted guests are all over at a local flea market today and won't be back until tea time." She stood and made her way to the kitchen. "Make yourself at home while I get you some breakfast."

After she left, Natalie squirmed a little on the uncomfortable relic. The settee was so tiny. How had Derek fit, let alone sleep? She couldn't sit five minutes in that thing, so she got up and started walking around the room.

The red-and-pink floral wallpaper was too formal and overwhelming for her taste. It made the room feel even more cramped. There were no pictures on the walls, except one, and it looked so woefully out of place that she gravitated toward it.

The frame was that cheap gold-plated style that chipped easily. She recognized Derek and the much slimmer version of Wes. The boys' heads were tilted toward a pretty woman with an asymmetrical bob sitting in the middle. She assumed that was their mother. A much younger version of Pops stood behind, his hand on Derek's shoulder.

While their poses were somewhat stiff, their smiles appeared to be genuine. They looked happy, but Natalie knew from experience how easy it was to fool the camera. She'd done it plenty of times.

Natalie turned as Janet entered the room. She set down a tray with coffee and muffins and walked over.

"Check out the high-top fades."

Janet laughed. "Certainly a throwback to simpler times, or at least it seemed like it back when we were kids."

"How old were they then?" she asked, pointing to Derek and Wes.

"In that picture, Wes is six and Derek is eight. Aren't they adorable?"

Natalie nodded her head in agreement. "They're both so cute," she exclaimed.

Of course, she favored Derek. His eyes had that innocent spark that few children seemed to have today.

"They look happy."

Janet shrugged. "As happy as they could be growing up at Pinecrest. It's cleaned up now, but it was rough around there in the '80s and early '90s."

"I once knew someone who grew up there. The stories he told me gave me nightmares for a while."

Natalie started to tell her about Jamal but then she'd

have to go into how she became a psychologist and why she wasn't one now.

It was bad enough that Janet had recognized her from her ice-skating days. She seemed to be the curious type, but not in a spiteful way, and Natalie thought that under different circumstances they would probably be friends.

Natalie turned toward the photo and studied Derek's mom. What kind of woman would abandon her husband and two sons?

"She was pretty, wasn't she?" Janet commented. "Too pretty for her own good."

"What happened to her?"

Janet shrugged. "Pops and Wes don't talk about her and I don't ask."

Natalie turned away, suddenly angry, and her heart went out to the three men whose lives had been devastated. She sat and poured herself a cup of coffee.

"Was Wes affected by his mother's abandonment?"

"It's an interesting question," Janet replied, refilling her mug. "I like to think that's why he is such a good provider, why he takes care of me and enjoys doing it, because he wasn't taken care of by his mother. It could have turned out worse."

Natalie sipped her coffee. "Derek and Wes were very lucky."

"It wasn't luck," Janet insisted. "It was good parenting. Pops is a good man."

"How often do you see him?" she asked.

"He comes over every week for Sunday dinner. All the guests are gone by then, so it's our time to unwind. He loves my roast turkey!"

"Does he ever ask about Derek? Talk about him?"

Janet hesitated as if she were unsure how much to reveal.

"No," she said finally. "But every now and then he'll look around the table like he knows it's not complete without Derek."

Natalie could empathize with Pops. Mealtimes were definitely better with family. She rarely ate at home, telling friends it was because she hated to clean. If you don't cook, it's really easy to keep the kitchen clean. And because they knew she was such a neat freak, they accepted her explanation.

But the real reason was that eating alone reminded her of all the nights she'd spent with her sitter instead of her parents. It reminded her of how alone she felt in the world.

She bit into her muffin and said a quick mental prayer for a speedy recovery for Pops and healing for the fractured Lansing family.

Janet's phone vibrated. "Excuse me," she said, quickly walking out of the room.

Natalie barely had time to swallow another bite of her muffin before Janet returned.

"That was Wes. Pops is waking up," she said excitedly. "We've got to get to the hospital right away."

Before Natalie could say anything, Janet had picked up the breakfast tray and walked into the kitchen.

"I was planning on going back to New York today," she revealed.

Janet's face fell. "Can you put it off a few hours? Derek wants you there."

"He said that?" Natalie asked, not bothering to hide the surprise on her face.

"I didn't speak to him directly, but Wes told me he did." Janet paused and gave her a strange look. "Why do you find that so hard to believe?"

Natalie's cheeks warmed under her inquisitive gaze. She'd forgotten that Janet was under the impression that she and Derek were together as a couple.

"I—I just figured Derek would only want his family around."

"Honey, the way he looks at you, you'd think you were his wife. The man clearly adores you."

Although Derek had told her he was falling hard for her, she wasn't so sure that equated adoration.

Perhaps his feelings for her were merely the result of a set of circumstances: a romantic location, mutual lust that could not be ignored and spur-of-the-moment emotional need. All those things could be the beginnings of love, but could not sustain a long-term relationship.

"Look, he even left the key to his car," Janet teased, dangling them in front of her. "Now that's a man who is in love."

On their way to the hospital, Janet yammered on and on about her "coupon wins," but Natalie hardly heard a word. All she could think about was Derek. Sure he trusted her with his car, but would he trust her with his heart?

There was a yellow taxi waiting outside the hospital and Natalie wished she had the guts to hop in, even though it would cost her a small fortune to take it all the way back to New York. Quickly, she nixed the idea. She'd promised she would stay until he and his father were reunited and she would keep her word, no matter what the outcome would be for her and Derek.

Her stomach was in knots as she followed Janet to the neurological unit on the top floor. Pops was out of intensive care and in a regular room. When they entered, the two brothers were sitting, flanking their father's hospital bed. A nurse was there, as well, checking vital signs.

Derek turned and his warm smile chased away her nerves. He stood, walked over and embraced her.

"I'm glad you're here," he whispered, his lips brushing the most sensitive part of her earlobe.

She hugged him back, wondering if he could feel her shiver in his arms, before they returned to Derek's place by the bed.

"How's he doing?" Natalie asked, watching Pops. Although he was still asleep, every few seconds his fingers would grasp the blankets.

"Stable," Wes said, accepting a kiss on the cheek from his wife. "The doctor said he would be waking up soon."

The nurse took the blood pressure cuff from her patient's arm and placed it back in the wire basket of the portable machine.

"His blood pressure is back within normal range," the nurse commented in a starched tone. "He'll be up and at 'em in no time."

"Then we're all in trouble." Wes quipped. His wisecrack had everyone laughing, even the nurse.

"You guys have been wonderful," Janet remarked.

"I'm sure staying with him by his bedside for hours had something to do with his quick recovery."

Derek waved her compliment aside. "We just did what needed to be done." Natalie saw him meet Wes's eyes. "We're family."

Wes cracked a smile. "It's about time you realized that, man!" He squeezed Janet's waist and she yelped. "It also helps to have two beautiful women at our sides, doesn't it, bro?"

Derek draped one arm around Natalie and looked down into her eyes. "More than you'll ever know," he murmured.

Their gazes locked and for once she wasn't uncomfortable with the fact that Wes and Janet were watching. She knew that the passion in his eyes wasn't for show, it was for real.

Pops grunted and everyone held their breath as he slowly turned toward Wes and opened his eyes.

He blinked. "Wes?"

Wes took his hand. "Yeah, Pops. I'm here."

He stared for a moment. "Where am I?"

"In the hospital," Wes replied.

"You fell in the parking lot of the high school," Janet added. "You gave us a pretty bad scare, but you're doing good now."

"Tell that to my head," he rasped weakly. "I feel like I've been run over by a truck." Moments later he turned his face toward Derek and his eyes widened.

"Hey, Pops."

His father started to lift his hand, but then took notice of the IV taped to the top of it. Derek reached over and gently squeezed his fingers, his lips curving into a half smile when his father squeezed back.

Pops looked him up and down. "How tall are you now?"

"Six-six," Derek responded proudly.

Pops mustered a low whistle. "Sit down. I'm likely to break my neck looking at you from this angle."

His smile faded at his father's gruff tone, but he obliged and pulled the chair alongside the bed, somehow managing to not crush his knees.

Natalie held her breath as both men remained silent, each one likely waiting for the other to make the first move toward reconciliation.

Pops spoke first. "I guess I can't slam the door in your face now, huh?"

The gruffness in his voice was still there, but it was softer and more round, and suddenly Natalie realized he was holding back tears.

Derek noticed, too, and gave him a worried smile. "You had every right. I've been such a jerk all these years."

Pops made a face and shook his head. "A father's supposed to set an example, not act like a child." A deep sigh rattled out of his chest. "No, I've made a lot of mistakes, too. More than I care to admit."

As he looked at his sons, he held out his other hand, and Wes took it. "But you both turned out to be fine young men, so I guess I did something right."

"You did more than do things right," Derek insisted, and Natalie could see the love he had for his father in his eyes. "You're the reason I'm where I am today."

Pops ran his tongue over his dry lips and cracked a grin. "Imagine that. Even though I can't shoot a free throw to save my life."

Derek put his hand on his father's shoulder. "Then I'll teach you."

"That's going to take a while," he replied, looking doubtful. "How long are you here for?"

"As long as you need me," Derek responded. There was a long pause, and Natalie said a mental prayer. "I want my family back…that is, if you'll have me."

Pops opened his arms and his eyes twinkled. "You're not too big to give your old man a hug, are you?"

The two men embraced, and it wasn't long before Wes encapsulated them both in a huge bear hug.

Natalie's eyes burned with happy tears for their reunion, as Janet clapped and clapped.

"Wes!" Pops called out in a muffled, panicked voice. "Break the huddle before I pass out!"

Both brothers stepped back to give their father some room to breathe, and saw that he was grinning.

"Gotcha!"

Everyone laughed with relief.

"I'd forgotten how much he loved to play practical jokes on us." Derek smirked.

"Just for that, you've got to promise to take your medicine. No more passing out in the parking lot," Wes scolded lightly. "You damn near gave *me* a heart attack."

"You just get well," Derek added. "We've got a lot of catching up to do."

"Indeed," Pops replied. "I see you're still chasing women!"

Derek draped his arm around Natalie and kissed her on the top of her head. "Only one, Pops. Only one."

Her body warmed as Derek tugged her even closer.

"This is Natalie, and she was the one who helped me realize I needed to change."

"A good woman will do that," Pops replied, nodding approvingly as Natalie stepped forward and kissed him on his cheek. "Hold on to her, Derek. Treasure her every day, as if it were your last."

Something electrifying crossed between them as Derek stared into her eyes, and she felt like she was the only person in the world. And the only woman for him.

"You can count on it, Pops."

A nurse burst into the room announcing it was almost time for Pops to have lunch and then a nap.

"But I just woke up!" he complained.

"Remember your promise," Wes warned.

"Okay, okay," he grumbled good-naturedly. "I want to get out of here, too." He looked around. "I don't think Medicare will pay for a private room."

Derek patted his shoulder. "Don't worry, Pops. I got this. I want you to rest and recuperate in the best surroundings possible."

"It's about time you put that money to good use!"

Natalie glanced at Derek, but he took his father's obvious jab at his lifestyle in stride. She was glad he didn't take offense, and it was clear that behind the criticism was a man who truly loved and missed his son.

Wes and Derek talked and laughed until the lunch tray was served and Pops shooed them all off so he could eat in peace and quiet. They left, promising to come back and visit later in the evening.

When they stepped out into the hall, Wes clapped Derek on the back. "I'm glad you and Pops are going to work things out."

"Me, too." He squeezed Natalie's hand. "I've got a lot of lost time to make up for, but I'm ready."

Wes yawned so loudly the nurses glared at him. "Speaking of time. I think it's about time for me to take a nap myself."

Janet shot him an annoyed glance. "And I have to go back and get ready for tea. Let's get out of here."

The four of them took the elevators to the front entrance of the hospital.

"What are you guys going to do?" Janet asked.

Natalie needed to go back to Belle Amour to pick up her bag. The reunion of the Lansing men was a success. As much as she didn't want to leave, it was time for her to go home. She opened her mouth to inform everyone of her plans, but Derek beat her to it.

"I'm going to show Natalie a little more of Baker's Falls. Don't wait up."

In her eyes? Only questions.

In his? Unknown surprises.

And when he looped his arm through hers, she went willingly, led only by her heart.

Derek could not believe his good fortune as he steered the Jeep toward the center of town, heady from the emotional events of the day. Pops forgave him, he had the woman he loved by his side and in a couple of days he would be back on the basketball court.

The trouble was he wasn't sure that's where he belonged anymore.

Although he'd promised his father to be there as long as he needed him, he was under contract to the New York Skylarks. He had a job to do. Pops would understand.

Wouldn't he?

The windows were cranked open, the unseasonably warm spring air caressing their faces, ruffling their hair, making him yearn for the ease of summer, when all concerns about the future seemed to disappear.

Hold on to her, Derek. Treasure her every day, as if it were your last.

Right now, he wanted to pretend it was summer. He didn't want to think about the future. It was the perfect day for a drive, and the perfect day to forget.

The hospital was only a few miles from the town. The shops surrounding the square were a little crowded, but the atmosphere was still what the local chamber of commerce described as "quaint" or "homespun." Growing up, he'd thought Baker's Falls was just plain boring. But now he was surprised to find he was excited to share the town with Natalie.

He glanced over at her. She was being unusually quiet this afternoon, even at the hospital, although he suspected that was out of respect for his family. Hopefully she wasn't regretting all the time they'd spent together the past few days.

"How about a picnic by the falls?" he asked, maneuvering the car into a parking spot.

She nodded and he drank in the smile that reached her eyes.

Taking her hand, he led them into a gourmet food store and coffee bar. The place was set up like an old-fashioned general store with wide-planked pine floors and country decorations. The scent of coffee beans, maple syrup and candles wafted through the air.

For their picnic lunch, they chose apple-pecan chicken salad on croissants, pita chips and chocolate-chip cookies for dessert. Derek grabbed a bottle of white wine. He had a lot to celebrate today.

"There are seven falls in the area," Derek said once they were back in the car. "And I'm going to take you to my favorite one."

Natalie said little as they drove the short distance to the falls, and Derek started to worry. It was as if she had something she wanted to tell him, but she was just waiting for the right time. He tried to forget that she'd never told him her feelings about him, but that was getting increasingly hard to do.

Maybe today would be the day.

He knew exactly how he felt about her.

He loved her.

Yet the way she was acting right now wasn't very loving. It was almost as if she were trying to distance herself from him.

He rubbed his thumb against his temple.

Would he ever figure women out?

"This particular waterfall is a little hard to get to,"

he said, glancing down at Natalie's sneakered feet. "I'm glad you have your walking shoes on today, not those high heels. Even though you did look very sexy in them yesterday."

She smiled and seemed surprised that he remembered. Her slender legs wrapped around his waist, drawing him into her core, possessing him fully, was something he never wanted to forget.

He pulled off the road, the tires crunching gravel. Derek could hear the roar of the waterfall even before he opened the door. Natalie got out and grabbed the lunch while he took a blanket from the back and shoved it in the crook of his arm.

"I can hear the waterfall," Natalie commented, looking around. "I just can't see it."

Derek pointed straight ahead. "There's a path to it right over there. Follow me and watch your step."

The roar of the falls grew louder and louder, and the dense forest seemed to part itself in two as they walked the narrow dirt path, studded with exposed tree limbs.

In a short time the flat path ended abruptly at an uphill mix of rocks. He climbed up first, set down the blanket and reached to assist Natalie.

When she reached the top, he set the bags on the blanket, gathered her into his arms and kissed her. The sweetness of her lips made him want to do more, made him love her as he'd never loved himself.

"I've wanted to do that for hours," he muttered, inhaling the lush apricot scent of her hair. He tilted her head back and his lips sought hers once again, fed hungrily as she cleaved her body against his.

"Derek," she said, pulling her face away. "What about the falls?"

She turned, and he kept his arms looped around her small waist, needing to keep her close to him.

As they both looked on, he was struck again by the natural wonder in front of him; the water cascading like a bride's veil, cut in two by glacial rocks and boulders. It spilled over the edge, flowing easily, before crashing into the pool of water below and merging into the narrow stream.

Where was the water's final destination? he wondered.

A lake? The Atlantic Ocean?

What was his?

Natalie sucked in a breath. "It's beautiful."

Her voice was round with awe and he exhaled in relief. She was a city girl, a born-and-bred New Yorker, that he wasn't sure she would like it. He was glad he'd brought her here.

Derek nodded. "As beautiful as they are, there's an unfortunate story behind these falls."

She turned to face him, her eyes dark. "Tell me about it."

He bent and spread the blanket over the flat, brown shale. When he was finished, he sat and offered his hand to Natalie. She knelt beside him and opened up the paper sacks.

"I don't know if it's true or not," Derek began, unscrewing the cap from the wine bottle. "But the story I always heard was that a young man and his new bride were exploring the area. They were trying to cross the river when they were both swept away and over the falls to their deaths."

"That's horrible," Natalie said with a shudder, tucking her legs under her. "And sad, too."

Derek shrugged and poured wine into the coffee cups he'd picked up from the store, and handed her one.

"Love hurts," he said wryly with a gestured toast, keeping his voice light. But inside, the words lodged like a rock in his brain, and he believed them because he'd experienced it so much.

The sound of the falls grew louder in his ears as he waited for her to touch his cup to hers.

But she never did and instead took a sip of wine, keeping her eyes on him.

"Love doesn't have to hurt, Derek," Natalie said quietly, setting down her cup. "It can heal, if you let it."

Her words stunned him and he silently accepted the sandwich she handed him, and the knowledge that she was right.

Yet he didn't know what required more courage. Loving someone? Or allowing love the time it needed to work its way into all the cracks and crevices of his broken heart, making it whole again?

He wasn't sure he was brave enough to do both.

Though he wasn't really hungry, he opened the wrapping and took a bite. The chicken salad, probably delicious on any other day, tasted bland on his tongue as it went down hard against the lump in his throat.

They ate in silence and kept their eyes on the falls. Derek's mind churned like the water hitting the rocks, flowing out into the unknown. As with the couple in the ancient legend, he and Natalie were crossing over to something different—unexplored territory. He wasn't sure if the feelings they had for each other, so new and unspoiled, would survive the journey.

Finishing his sandwich, he balled up the empty wrapping and stuffed it in the sack.

"I'm so glad you and your dad are speaking again."

He nodded, felt a frown tug at his lips. "I'm just sorry I waited so long. I don't know why I did, but I guess I was afraid."

"Of what?" she asked before biting into a pita chip.

"Not so much that we wouldn't reconcile, but that we would. Crazy, huh?"

She shook her head. "It's normal. You weren't sure how Wes or your father would react to your intentions. Thankfully, everything turned out well."

He held up his cup in a toast. "Thanks to you. You gave me the kick in the pants that I needed."

This time she toasted back, lifting his heart and his spirits.

They sipped their wine as leaves crinkled and waved above them. He looked into her eyes, gaining strength for what he was about to say.

"You know, when I play basketball..." he began, wishing he had one in his hands to calm his nerves. "I know exactly what to do. I'm expected to control the ball, ensuring it gets to the right players. The coach sets his game plan and I help him execute it to the best of my ability.

"But in a relationship, I don't know what's expected

of me. There *is* no game plan. There's only my heart… and how I feel."

He took her hand, opened her palm and moved his lips over the surface. "I've only known you a short while, but you've already made a huge impact in my life," he murmured, his eyes closed. "So I can't figure out why such an amazing woman like you isn't snatched up yet."

Her eyes widened and she trembled under his touch. "Believe it or not, I haven't had the time for a relationship."

He lifted his head from her palm and pulled her onto his lap, groaning as her soft buttocks nestled against him.

He cradled her close. "Make time for one," he commanded, lowering his lips inches above hers. "With me."

When he tried to kiss her, she pulled roughly away and stood. "What kind of a relationship could we have, Derek?" she asked, wiping her hands down the front of her pants, as if he were a crumb she was trying to remove from her clothes.

He jumped to his feet. "I don't have a specific plan. Can't we just figure it out along the way?"

She shook her head. "I don't see how it would work. We both travel so much. We both love our careers. You said so yourself—you weren't sure you could give it up for a woman. What changed your mind?"

"I fell in love with you, that's what changed it!" he declared, hating that they were arguing and confused at how everything had changed so quickly. "I want to build a life with you."

"That's just it, Derek. You can't build a life with someone when you're still trying to pick up the pieces from your old life. You need to concentrate on healing and rebuilding your relationship with your family. Not starting one with me."

He went to her, gripping her shoulders lightly.

"Can't I have both? Can't we?"

He tried to pull her toward him, but she twisted away, taking his heart with her.

"Not people like us. We're too driven, too focused. And we have too many people depending on us to make the right choices."

He started to argue when his cell phone rang. When he saw who it was, he groaned but answered anyway.

"Yeah, what's up?" he said harshly, turning his back on Natalie and walking away.

"Where are you?" Tony snapped. "I've been trying to reach you for days."

Derek had purposely ignored the calls from his manager and he waited until he was out of earshot of Natalie before responding.

"I came back home. I'm here with that life coach you hired."

"Is she helping you?" Tony asked.

He looked back at Natalie, where she stood, with her hands on her hips, questions in her eyes. "Yeah, she's helping me."

She's just not loving me.

The pain of rejection squeezed in his chest and he

barely heard Tony yammering at him. "You've got to come back to New York right away. Tonight, in fact."

His mind suddenly snapped to attention. "Why? My suspension doesn't end till Tuesday. I was planning on staying here through the weekend. My dad..."

His voice trailed off and he was glad he shut up. He didn't want Tony to know about his reconciliation with his family or Pop's being in the hospital. Tony would turn it around into a publicity ploy, cheapen all the emotion Derek took from being forgiven, tarnishing everything he and Natalie had worked so hard to fix.

Now he was on his own.

"You have a very important meeting tonight, or did you forget?

Derek slapped his hand on his forehead. In light of everything else that happened, he had forgotten. Damn Tony for calling and reminding him.

"You can't miss it. You promised you'd be there. Can I count on you?"

He shut his eyes, Natalie's words floating through his mind.

We have too many people depending on us to make the right choices.

"Yeah," he muttered, opening his eyes. "I'll be there."

He hit the end button. This meeting that required his attendance had been planned weeks earlier, but it couldn't have happened at a worse time. Things with Pops and Wes were still new, still fragile. Plus he and Natalie hadn't had a chance to talk things over.

But it couldn't be helped now. His brother and father

knew who he was, what he was all about. He hoped and prayed they would understand.

This was who he was!

As for Natalie, from the way she was acting, it appeared that she didn't love him anyway.

He sucked in a deep breath, held it as long as he could. When he exhaled, he rocked back on his feet, knowing that he'd have to let Natalie go, too.

He'd been ready to commit to her, yet it was obvious she didn't feel the same way. He no longer needed to worry about making a choice where she was concerned. She'd made it for him.

Derek pushed his disappointment and heartache aside for the moment, walked back and started to pack everything up.

"Is there anything wrong?" she asked.

"No, but I have to go back to New York," he said, folding the blanket over his arm. "Right now."

"Now?" Her voice was a mixture of hurt and confusion. "Who was that?"

"Just a friend," he replied, avoiding her eyes. "Come on, let's go."

He strode away without waiting for her to respond, slid down the rocky embankment, then held out his hand to help her safely down.

When her feet hit the hard dirt, he took off down the path, stopping only when she grabbed his arm.

"But what about your father? He's still recovering. You promised him you'd be there for him."

"Don't you think I know that?" His voice seemed to echo through the forest, the pain in it reverberated off the tree bark and etched his face, held in by pride and the thick canopy of leaves.

He stalked off again, hastily threw everything onto the backseat and jumped in the car, drumming his fingers on the steering wheel impatiently. If he got to the airport right away, he'd have enough time to fly home and get changed before the meeting.

Natalie opened the door and got in. He started the Jeep and the wheels spun in the gravel as he sped off the embankment and onto the main road.

"What about your luggage?"

There was no way he was going back to Belle Amour now. What explanation would he give to Wes?

"Bring it with you, will you?"

"You mean I'm not going with you?" Natalie asked.

Much as he wanted her to be with him, Derek knew he had to face this alone. "You hate flying, remember? I'm going to leave the car with you, so you can drive back to New York on your own."

Natalie didn't say a word the entire drive to the airport, and Derek was secretly relieved. Talking led to questions, and right now, he wasn't ready to provide the answers she wanted, because he wasn't sure of the outcome.

He wanted to show Natalie, his family and the world that he could be different. But mostly, he wanted to prove it to himself, and he knew tonight may be his only chance.

When they arrived at the terminal, Derek parked and got out of the car. He left it running and met Natalie on the passenger side.

She reluctantly took the hand he offered and stepped out. He was leaving her with virtually no explanation. Some prince he turned out to be, he thought.

"Why are you doing this?" she asked quietly.

His head tilted up and he searched the clouds, wishing he could make her understand.

"An opportunity," he replied firmly, and he could tell by the look on her face that she knew his mind was made up.

He took both her hands in his. "Do you ever miss ice skating?"

She tilted her head in surprise. "I used to," she admitted. "But not anymore. It's no longer who I am."

He paused for a long time. "You're lucky."

Natalie blinked hard and he knew she was about to cry. So he walked away from her and into a place deep inside himself.

This is the last time.

I promise.

Chapter 12

"Way to go, Ice Queen!" she muttered, wiping her tears away with one hand as she angled Derek's car out of the parking lot and onto the main road. She'd had the chance to tell Derek that she loved him, now that chance was gone. Perhaps forever.

What was wrong with her?

For a while she drove around mindlessly. Her brain was in a fog, trying to piece together the events of the afternoon, as she struggled to cope with her emotions.

Finally she switched on the vehicle's GPS system. Derek was in such a hurry to hop in his plane and get out of town that he'd forgotten to tell her how to get back to Belle Amour.

The question she wanted to know was what had

drawn him back to New York so urgently. What was behind this so-called "opportunity"?

Although she felt sure in her heart that he wasn't fleeing to another woman, when she checked her phone, there were no calls or texts from him. She didn't even know if she'd hear from him when he got home.

Natalie glanced at the clock on the dashboard. It was just after 4:00 p.m. She could pick up her bag, hit the highway and be back in her own bed sometime this evening.

Or at Derek's apartment.

For a moment she considered stopping by the hospital to tell Derek's father what was going on, but she quickly dismissed the thought as silly.

It wasn't her place to tell him anything. She'd just met the man for the first time today. She wasn't family. She was an outsider. But mostly, she was afraid she would be blamed for Derek leaving Baker's Falls. Her heart lurched at the memory of his tender kisses and his declaration of his love came roaring back.

She gripped the steering wheel even tighter. It *was* her fault that he wasn't sitting beside her right now. She'd rejected him, and she didn't need to put on her psychologist cap to know that no man stuck around when the woman he loved rejected him.

She couldn't run away from the facts. Before she left for New York, she had to go back and tell Wes and Pops the truth.

When she arrived at Belle Amour, she couldn't help but be disappointed to see Wes's truck in the driveway. A small part of her had hoped he wouldn't be home.

Don't be such a coward, she told herself.

He was sitting on the porch stairs with an old metal colander, snapping green beans. Natalie almost laughed out loud. Janet sure knew how to get her man to help her in the kitchen.

Wes called out to her. "Janet's put me to work. She wants to bring Sunday dinner to Pops tomorrow, so we're starting to get everything ready now."

He nodded as she sank next to him. "You're back early. Where's Derek?"

She stared out at the rosebushes that lined the yard. "He flew back to New York, and I'm not sure if he's ever coming back."

Wes stopped midsnap. "What happened?"

The red-and-pink roses were blurry now. "That's the problem. I don't know. But I think I may have an idea."

She wiped a tear away, ashamed to be crying in front of a man she hardly knew. "He left because of me."

Wes set the colander aside and turned toward her. "What did he say?"

She told him about being at the falls, and how he got a call from a "friend" and that when he'd hung up, he'd announced he had to go back to New York.

"He said he had an opportunity. But I know he never would have left if I had told him how I felt about him."

Wes grunted and picked up the colander. He started snapping beans again.

"What?" she asked, slightly hurt that he seemed to be ignoring her plight. "What did I say?"

His beefy hands paused. "I think you're reading too much into this. Derek *has* changed. He'll be back."

She lowered her head in shame. “I hope you’re right.”

“Of course I’m right,” he replied with a smile. He nudged her with his elbow. “Have a little faith.”

She chuckled a little, at herself mostly, because if she didn’t laugh, she would cry.

Here she was, Derek’s life coach, the person who was hired to help him overcome his past and get on the right track, and she was giving up on him.

Perhaps she was in the wrong profession. But that wasn’t it, either. The problem was that she’d gotten personally involved with her client. Lost her head, lost her heart, and now she’d lost her will.

“I need to get back to New York, too. Thank goodness Derek left me his car. I was going to go tonight.”

Wes cut her off and shot her a look. “Tonight? It’ll be dark soon.” He rolled his eyes. “And now I’m starting to sound like your mother.”

Natalie laughed. Wes really was a sweet guy. Janet was so lucky to have him.

“But seriously, just stay another night, okay?” he said, shaking a bean at her. “Things will look better in the morning.”

“Okay. You’re right. It is getting too late to drive home safely.”

After politely refusing dinner, Natalie excused herself and went upstairs. She slipped out of her clothes and went to choose a nightgown when she realized she didn’t have any clean ones.

She spotted Derek’s carry-on next to the armoire. Unzipping it, she found one of his clean shirts and slipped it on. She walked into the bathroom for a look and despite her somber mood, she couldn't help but giggle. His shirt was so large it draped to her knees.

After pulling the shades, she slipped under the covers. She bunched Derek's shirt up in her fist and brought it to her nose. It even smelled like him. Spicy and strong and sexy. That's when the loneliness hit her.

"Love hurts," she whispered into her pillow as she fell into a deep yet restless sleep.

Derek stepped out of the black stretch limo, ignored the flashbulbs clicking, the jealous stares held back by red-velvet ropes, and checked his watch. It was 9:00 p.m. sharp. For once, he was right on time.

He only wished Natalie was there to see him dressed in a black designer suit and a deep purple button-down shirt, instead of his everyday clothes. It had only been a few hours since he'd left Baker's Falls, and already he missed her terribly.

Two bouncers accompanied him as he walked the red carpet and into the club where a beautiful girl stood waiting by the door.

"Welcome back, Mr. Lansing."

He nodded and followed her as she escorted him upstairs to the VIP lounge.

Heads looked up with interest as he stepped into the room. Derek shivered a little, even though he wasn't cold. The club was located in a converted warehouse, and there always seemed to be an unseemly chill in the air.

The VIP area used to be administrative offices, where the company executives could look down on the workers. The original glass had been replaced with one-way glass, so guests could spy on the people below as they danced and writhed to the music.

He stepped to the window and gazed at the DJ up in a booth like a watchman's tower where he controlled the crowd with beats and rhyme and musical chaos. His eyes moved over the plasma televisions embedded in the walls that showed the sweaty, youthful faces made grotesque by the flash of the strobe lights.

God, he was tired of this scene.

The music that normally energized him suddenly repulsed him and he had to fight the urge to clap his hands over his ears.

A man approached him, short and impeccably dressed. His tanned skin was bought, not natural. Neither were his teeth, which gleamed white with implants.

"Derek!" the man shouted over the din of the music. "Mickey Stanluca. It's a pleasure to finally meet you," he said a little too enthusiastically, offering his hand.

Derek shook it, but when he released his grip, his hand felt slimy, even though his palms were completely dry.

So this was the elusive Mr. Stanluca, owner of the club. He was rarely seen, yet everyone knew who he was. Tony had told him that Mickey was a big fan and wanted to meet him.

"I've spent many a night watching you courtside

while you worked your magic for our New York Sky-larks. Perhaps you noticed me?"

Derek arched an eyebrow and took a step back. Was the man coming on to him, or was he just crazy? He shook his head and plastered on a polite smile, even though he was annoyed. He cursed Tony inwardly for setting up a meeting that was looking like a complete waste of his time.

"No, I'm afraid I didn't. When I'm on the court, all I can think about is the ball and doing whatever I can to help my team win."

Mickey chuckled, but for some reason, Derek got the feeling he was not amused, that he wanted to be noticed.

"Of course, of course," he said. "Come, let's sit down."

There were a number of attractive females in the room, all with knowing smiles on their faces. He recognized a few of them, but couldn't remember their names. At the time, it didn't matter. But now his face flushed with shame.

They were just two consenting adults having a little fun. For what? So they could stare at each other across a room?

Strangers then.

Strangers now.

Derek jerked his attention back to Mickey as they sat across from each other on black leather sofas.

"What's your poison?" he said, gesturing toward the well-appointed bar.

He waved his offer away. "Just a club soda for me,"

he responded, wanting to have all his wits about him tonight.

"With you drinking like that, my Scotch will go down even smoother," he joked, gesturing to a waiter.

They made small talk as they waited for their drinks.

Here and there, Derek saw couples huddled up, making him yearn even more for Natalie, stirring up the guilt he felt for leaving her, and his father.

Even though she'd rejected him, he was still drawn to her, the feistiness that lay beneath her quiet demeanor.

When they arrived, Mickey held his glass in a toast.

"To new beginnings."

Derek reluctantly clicked his glass against Mickey's, who promptly downed the contents in a couple of seconds.

"When I contacted Tony with my plan and told him about it, he told me you were a man who liked to party." Mickey laughed. "On your off hours, that is." He laughed again, insinuating that Derek partied twenty-four hours a day.

I'm not like that, he wanted to scream. Although admittedly there were some nights when he got home that he felt as though he'd been carousing all day, instead of just a few hours. Those were the days when something triggered a feeling deep inside and all he'd wanted to do was tamp it down and throw ashes on the memory, so he could finally forget.

The next day when he woke up, he knew he'd tricked himself. The memories never went away. The feelings were stored inside his heart, and it was only a matter of time before they were released again.

"I used to be..." he managed to say, but the words felt foreign.

Mickey squinted at him and then went on talking as if he hadn't heard. "You're one of our best customers."

Derek knew it was not just a compliment—it was true. He didn't even want to think about the thousands of dollars he'd spent at this particular club. It was the perfect escape. The booze and the music drowned out the pain, while the women falling all over him were a balm to his ego, especially on the rare days when the Skylarks lost.

"This is a fun little spot," he remarked, because it was true. He just wasn't into it anymore. "But it's been a while since I've been here."

"So are you interested in buying it?"

Derek stared at the man, openmouthed. "What are you talking about?"

"I'm looking for a buyer for this place. I've got my hands in a lot of different businesses, but now I'm trying to sell off a few of them." Mickey lifted his glass. "To the right person, of course."

Derek took a sip of club soda. "Why?"

"Two words. Abu Dhabi."

Derek nodded. He had an interest in international business and had heard about the second largest city of the United Arab Emirates, known also as one of the richest cities in the world. In addition, Abu Dhabi was the capital of the region.

"It's hip, it's cosmopolitan, and a mecca for the new glitterati," Mickey continued. "Plus the climate is favorable for these old bones." He laughed as he took a yellow envelope from inside his suit coat and placed it on the glass table between them.

"I'm sure you'll find the terms quite favorable."

Derek opened the documents. The room was quite dark, so he dug his cell phone out of his pocket to illuminate the pages. He read quickly, scanning for the most important thing—the price. His eyes widened when he found it.

Mickey watched his reaction and chuckled. "I see you agree. Quite favorable, yes?"

He tapped his finger against the envelope. "You'll find the appraisal in there, as well. This place has been inspected from top to bottom and there are no violations. The liquor license is sound and up-to-date."

Derek reviewed the additional paperwork, his eyes widening, not in surprise but in suspicion.

He pointed to the appraisal. "The club is worth five times what you're selling it for. Care to tell me why you're off-loading it so cheaply?"

Mickey steepled his fingers and put his elbows on his knees. He leaned forward, so he wouldn't need to raise his voice over the din of the music.

"I wanted to keep the barrier to entry lower," he explained. "I know you are a fairly cautious investor. Other than your car, your plane and your apartment, you own very little for a man your age and of your prominence."

"So what?" Derek retorted, a little peeved that the man insinuated he needed more things than he already had.

"You can't play basketball forever."

Mickey's words hit him square in the gut and he leaned back against the couch. He was right. It was only a matter of time before he got injured. Basketball was a grueling sport and although he was in top physical condition, he knew it wouldn't last.

Neither would the lucrative sponsorship deals he currently enjoyed. Eventually they'd run out, too.

Mickey watched him. "If you're interested, I need your answer in twenty-four hours. You're my first choice to take over this place, but I do have someone else in mind if you turn me down."

Derek got up out of his seat and stood at the window. He peered down at the gyrating crowd below.

Did he really want to run himself into the ground before his prime? He loved basketball. It was the game that tore his family apart and conversely brought it back together when he'd met Natalie. And it was the game that could end everything he was trying to build with her.

Did he really want that?

The bass pumped in time with the beat of his heart.

"I don't need twenty-four hours," he said, returning to the table. He remained standing as he folded the documents and slipped them back inside the envelope. "The answer is no."

Mickey reeled back in surprise. "You're missing the opportunity of a lifetime!"

"No," Derek assured him. "I'm creating another one."

And he walked out of the club and hailed a cab. Once inside, he made a call. Tony picked up on the first ring.

"Hey, how'd it go with Mickey?" Tony said cheerfully.

"It went great," Derek replied. "You're fired."

Click.

The second phone call was more difficult, but necessary. When it was done, he felt peaceful and had no regrets, giving him the courage he needed for the journey ahead.

Natalie's bag was packed and stowed in the Jeep, but she couldn't leave and go back to New York just yet. Not until she told someone how she felt about Derek.

And that someone was Pops.

Somehow she'd also find a way to break it to him gently that Derek was gone.

She stood just outside his hospital room, her back pressed against the wall, trying to muster up enough courage to go in.

Although visiting hours had begun, she wasn't sure Pops was awake yet, although she could hear the boisterous voices of two sports announcers from his television.

A nutritional aide approached, carrying a tray. Her bored frown morphed into a polite smile when she saw Natalie standing there, likely assuming she was a relative of the patient.

Without thinking, Natalie pushed herself off the

wall and followed her. She waited inside the room and watched the aide set the tray on the table and push it over the bed.

"Good morning!" Natalie said when the aide left.

"Breakfast and a beautiful lady," Pops exclaimed, pressing one button to lower the volume on the television and another to raise the bed to a sitting position. "Just what the doctor ordered."

She didn't know exactly how old Pops was—she guessed between sixty-five and seventy—yet he was still handsome. His broad, toothy grin made her feel special.

Natalie's cheeks warmed. "You're a flirt, just like Derek."

"Who do you think he learned it from?" he said, lifting the aluminum cover off the plate. "Mmm. Pancakes and sausage. They keep feeding me like this and I'll leave here with a heart attack instead of a head concussion."

She pulled a plastic chair over and sat. "How are you feeling today?"

"They took the IV out, so I no longer feel like a puppet on a string. Other than a nagging headache, I'm doing fine. They said they'd kick me out in a few days, and believe me, I can't wait to get home and sleep in my own bed."

He unwrapped the plastic cutlery and tucked a napkin on his lap. "You don't mind if I eat, do you?"

When she shook her head, he began to cut his pancakes.

"Where is my son, anyway?"

She hated the tears that burned her eyes and threatened to fall, exposing her emotions before she was ready. On the drive over, she'd run through a litany of positive affirmations in her mind designed to help her stay strong.

Now, she couldn't remember the healing words, couldn't stop regretting that she had withdrawn her heart from Derek. "That's what I came to talk to you about. He's gone back to New York and I think it's all my fault."

Pops stopped chewing for a second and then quickly swallowed, recognition dawning on his face.

"That's what I thought, too."

"What do you mean?" she asked, surprised that he didn't seem disappointed or worried by what she'd just told him.

He put his fork on the tray, concern etched in the lines surrounding his eyes.

"All those years I spent away from my son, I blamed myself." He reached for her hand. "But you know what I learned during that time?"

She shook her head.

"Blaming yourself is a lot easier than loving the person who hurt you."

Tears sprang to her eyes. Such wise advice. It was the type of counsel she would have given her patients when she was a psychologist.

How quickly she'd forgotten.

"But how do you stop blaming yourself?" she asked, needing his perspective.

Pops chuckled. "Now that's the interesting part. I don't know."

He stirred two sugars into his coffee. "But now that Derek is back in my life, I'd rather work on loving him and building a relationship, than blaming myself, and figuring out how to do both along the way."

She raised her eyebrows. "Trial and error."

"That's what life and love is about, isn't it?" He nodded and his voice took on a more serious tone. "Derek and I both wasted a lot of years. That's time we'll never get back."

She squeezed his hand, cold and gnarled with veins, and his upper lip quivered.

"I'm not a young man anymore. I'm not too proud to mop floors for a living, never was. But I was always too proud to tell my sons that I loved them. Not anymore."

I wish I had that kind of courage.

He looked her straight in the eyes, as if he could read her thoughts.

"Natalie, if there's something important that you need to tell my son, don't wait. Just open your mouth and let your heart speak for you."

His words and the determination in his eyes warmed her, and she leaned back in her chair with amazement.

"Derek is so lucky to have you for a father."

Pops bowed halfway. "Why thank you, miss!"

She hesitated, not sure if she should pry. "What was he like as a kid?"

He laughed. "I used to call him Sir Bounce-A-Lot. He would never sit still, he was always moving. One day I gave him a basketball, with the hope that it would cure his fidgety ways, and the rest is history, and I've never regretted my decision."

"That's a great story!" Natalie responded with a smile. But Pops wasn't listening. His eyes were on the television set and he was frowning. Natalie followed his gaze and saw Derek's picture on the screen. She pushed the button on the side of the hospital bed to turn up the volume so they could hear what was being said.

"Derek Lansing is calling it quits. The popular power forward for the New York Skylarks announced his retirement from professional basketball today, effective at the end of the season. Lansing's playing, always off the charts for the bulk of his career, has been hit-or-miss for most of this season. He's coming off suspension and will be back on the court this week. When asked the reason for his retirement, Lansing declined to answer. But perhaps he's not giving up the game he loves and plays so well entirely. It's rumored he's entertaining offers to coach at the college level."

Pops whistled low, pressed a button, and the television went dark. Stunned at the news, they turned and looked at each other with shock in their eyes and the ultimate question in their minds. Why?

"I never thought in a million years he'd retire this soon, this young," Pops said, shaking his head as he pushed the table that held his breakfast to the other side of the bed. "That must have been why he left abruptly last night."

"Perhaps." Natalie wrung her hands in her lap. "I just hope he's okay. I hope nothing happened to him."

Derek suddenly walked into the room and they both jumped in surprise.

"That's the good news," he announced. "Something *did* happen to me. Something wonderful."

Derek went to Natalie and pulled her out of her chair.

"I fell in love with a woman who inspires me to want to be more than I am right now."

He reached over and gripped Pop's hand. "And I reunited with a father who forgave me after years of pain," he affirmed, clasping his arm around Natalie's shoulder. "And both of you are more important to me than anything else in this world."

The huge smile on Pop's face lit up the drab hospital room as he extended his arms toward Derek.

"I'm so proud of you, son."

Derek released her shoulder and the two men hugged for a long time. When they stopped, both had tears in their eyes, relieved that the layers of regret and years of estrangement had finally melted away.

"So what's the bad news?" Pops joked.

"Well…" Derek said slowly, trying to hide a smile. "Natalie is going to have to suffer through a trip to Tiffany's to shop for an engagement ring. That is, if she'll agree to marry me."

Tears welled in her eyes and she was speechless with joy.

But when he moved to kiss her, she quickly pulled away, and she could hardly bear the crestfallen look on his face. He thought she was rejecting him, but nothing could be further from the truth.

She placed her hands on his face, and she could feel him tremble as she traced the strong lines of his jaw.

It's now or never. Yet she was no longer afraid.

"A wise man once told me that when I couldn't find the words to tell someone how I felt, I should just let my heart speak for me."

She glanced down at Pops, her courage strengthened by his smile.

"What is your heart telling you?" Derek asked gently.

"That I love you," she whispered. "Because I do."

And this time when Derek moved to kiss her, she didn't step away, but fell into his arms and a future they would build, and figure out, together.

* * * * *